Roden Noel

Livingstone in Africa

Roden Noel

Livingstone in Africa

ISBN/EAN: 9783743347755

Manufactured in Europe, USA, Canada, Australia, Japa

Cover: Foto ©Raphael Reischuk / pixelio.de

Manufactured and distributed by brebook publishing software (www.brebook.com)

Roden Noel

Livingstone in Africa

LIVINGSTONE IN AFRICA.

LIVINGSTONE IN AFRICA.

BY

THE HON. RODEN NOEL.

LONDON:

SAMPSON LOW, MARSTON, LOW AND SEARLE,

CROWN BUILDINGS, FLEET STREET.

1874.

CHISWICK PRESS :—PRINTED BY WHITTINGHAM AND WILKINS,
TOOKS COURT, CHANCERY LANE.

PREFACE.

THERE is a disposition among some contemporary critics to debar the Poet from contemporary subjects. One critic alleges these to be essentially unpoetical. Another—more skilled in delicate distinctions, and priding himself on the adroitness with which, as it were, by a dexterous turn of the wrist, he can cause the fine edge of them to wound, without vulgarly and directly thrusting— might prefer to say, apropos of each writer in turn who chooses such themes, that "at any rate *this* writer has not shown how contemporary subjects may be made poetical"—which remark, however, the poet, if he be a poet, can afford to

treat simply as a piece of impertinence. He will
have adapted his workmanship, arrangement, and
mode of expression to the nature of his subject-
matter. Perchance the problem of conciliating
superfine collegians, or light skirmishers detached
from their main body in the shape of certain "ir-
responsible reviewers," and at the same time satis-
fying intelligent readers of poetry in general—
unephemeral critics, who are beyond the passing
fashion of a clique—may be a problem well-nigh
as insoluble as that of perpetual motion. But if
so, a poet should be prepared with contempt and
defiance only for the former. To me I confess it
appears that Past and Present are equally poetical,
when regarded and treated by a poet—equally
unpoetical when regarded and treated by a mere
versifier—though I am far from saying that every
particular time is fully as poetical as any other.
But the present time seems by no means deficient
in that respect. No age is heroic to its valet-de-
chambre; and every age has many valets-de-cham-
bre. If there is danger from vulgar and debasing

associations, and from fragmentary nearness, in the Present, which has not yet "orbed into the perfect star," there is equal danger from remoteness in the Past—few imaginations being indeed adequate satisfactorily to realize very different conditions of life and thought. The name of little flutterers, whose inanimate remains are strewn along the avenue that leads to the Temple of Fame, is Legion ; but pseudo-classical and pseudo-mediæval versifiers are surely not inadequately represented among them. Some indeed have failed in poetically representing what passed under their eyes, because the eyes of the soul were wanting—the Poet's second sight. Moreover, the genius of some true poets has proved more at home in those rarer, yet still to them living, regions of the Past. I do not think the age of Chaucer was much more poetical than the age of Victor Hugo and Tennyson: but Chaucer contrived to see and represent his age poetically: and though, perhaps, Tennyson's greatest works have dealt with ideal, romantic, or classical themes, he has shown

himself master also in setting contemporary life
to music. If Shakspeare wrote Julius Cæsar, he
also wrote Henry VIII.; and Hamlet is essentially
modern. Dante does not appear to have thought
his own age unpoetic, though himself the master
of ideal or spiritual creations. Dante, and Milton,
set the dominant theologies of their own day
to music; while Dante is full of allusions to
passing events. Homer did not endeavour to
reproduce classically correct imitations of the
poems he may have read in Egyptian papyri.
Gama, the hero of Camoens's epic, was still
alive when the poet was a boy; and Camoens
himself took part in adventures similar to those
which he relates—indeed he contrives to relate
what was actually happening in the Lusiad itself.
Dryden wrote of Contemporary Politics; Pope
sang the Rape of the Lock; Byron sang contemporary life in Childe Harold and Don Juan;
Wordsworth also in some of his greatest poems.
So did Campbell, Gray, and Goldsmith at their
best—while Scott, if he sang of chivalry, sang at

least of Scotland. The greatest work of Goethe is distinctly modern ; so are the works of Hugo and De Musset. Spenser, Chatterton, Landor, and Keats, on the other hand—may one not add Mr· Browning ?—breathe more freely in alien, or ideal, atmospheres ; but then they do themselves breathe there ; they do not merely simulate the accents of those who once did so.

That events of our own time may be treated poetically has been proved by our greatest poetess, Mrs. Browning ; although, partly from the fact that England as a nation has withdrawn herself more and more from active participation in events of cosmopolitan interest, our writers of verse have not recently invited attention to contemporary themes ; while studious readers have seemed disposed to discourage such attempts. But two or three genuine poets have quite lately made successful efforts to break through a somewhat vulgar, prosaic, and discreditable apathy—though it is one no doubt on which our fashionable *petite culture* very much plumes itself. In America we

have, for instance, Longfellow and Walt Whitman; while in England we have not only Arthur
Clough, and R. Buchanan, but also Mr. Swinburne,
who wrote recently the "Songs before Sunrise."
These poets at all events have proved that they
do not, from feeling their own impotence, desire
to insult their Mother-Age, and charge her with
all the responsibility of a defect, which after all
may not be of quite cosmical urgency. More
recently still, Mr. Alfred Austin seems to have
comically disproved his own somewhat juvenile
criticism on the futility of the age, and the con-
sequent inevitable futility of its poets, by himself
writing a really fine poem on contemporary events,
"Rome or Death."

However, in the following work I have the so
much desiderated advantage of *remoteness*—remoteness, if not in time, at least in place. Africa
is a long way off; Cook's tourists do not go to
Ujiji; and both men and nature in Africa are very
different from what they are immediately around
us—if that be an advantage. My object has been

to sing the *modern Explorer*—suggesting, dimly
it may be, the *Explorer*, or *Seeker*, in a wider
sense. In an oasis of the Sahara, and other re-
mote regions, a poem on this subject dawned on
me. It is a subject peculiarly modern, peculiarly
English, and as I believe peculiarly poetical ; one
destined, moreover, to be always interesting. Even
.the most jaded student, to whom life and nature
as he sees them are " flat, stale and unprofitable,"
must (one would fancy) be interested in the records
of exploration that are published from time to time
by great travellers. At any rate young persons,
and persons young-hearted, though no longer
young in years, are appealed to in my poem. I
have done my best : for its shortcomings, I must
appeal to the indulgence of such sympathetic
readers as these. If I shall have been enabled to
impart to them any measure of elevated enjoyment,
I shall be satisfied. The *Explorer in Africa*, a
most ancient, till yesterday almost unknown land ;
North of which lies Egypt ; South of which lies
Ethiopia, and all her still half-hidden marvels !

the very regions of earthly mystery; yet how profoundly and pathetically human after all in their
strange disclosures !

Poets used to sing of heroes, and great actions.
I do not know why they should now only spin
subtle cobwebs out of their own insides. Nor,
however, do I know how long a period must elapse,
according to the dogmas of " culture," before a
mere dead man may, (by virtue of mischievous
worshipping and myth-making propensities unfortunately inherent in our race,) be considered
as fairly canonized—elevated to the dignity of
" a hero." But for my part, I used to think
Livingstone a true hero while he was alive; and
my opinion of him is only not changed now
that he is dead. Our two Florences, Florence
Nightingale, and Florence Lady Baker, moreover,
appear to me to be heroines—though both of
them (one is glad to know) are still alive. Nor
should those brave exploring ladies, the Dutch
Miss Tinnés, be forgotten here. At any rate, the
figure of David Livingstone admirably fills the
shadowy, but colossal outlines of the Explorer.

I have endeavoured to represent his life, adventures, character and aims, with the accuracy of fact; though in one instance I have imagined a scene characteristic of a phase of African experience, which would otherwise have remained unillustrated; but this is a kind of experience which Livingstone might easily have passed through personally; and of course I have exercised a privilege of selection. The scene of the first Cantos is laid at Ujiji on Lake Tanganyika; where Livingstone has been driven back by the malice or cowardice of some who followed him, when on the eve, as he believed, of solving for ever those grand problems of geography, which have engaged the world's attention from earliest ages.

He has arrived ill, worn-out, aged, destitute; to find the goods on which he depended dissipated by the rascal to whom they had unfortunately been entrusted; and he could, (suffering as he was from his old disease, dysentery,) hardly have held out much longer, had not Mr. Stanley so gallantly and unexpectedly relieved him.

(1871). I imagine him sitting on the open veran-
dah of his tembé, looking eastward, as Stanley
describes him; while evening deepens, and then
night—the night preceding Stanley's arrival. I
suppose that — like those constellations, with
which he is so familiar—the salient features of
his whole life pass successively before him in his
solitude; while he meditates at leisure upon the
people and scenes he has witnessed; wonders
what people and scenes are yet to be divulged
for him; speculating, moreover, on those long-
vexed, fascinating problems, suggested by history,
geography, and science, in connection with his
beloved continent. But his chief concern—though
he takes a very humane and broad interest in all—
is the future of the people, among whom he has
so long lived: he is a profoundly sincere Christian missionary—a philanthropist in the best and
widest sense—with heart bleeding for all the
ignorance, darkness, and misery, which he sees
around him; thirsting to devise the best possible
means for the salvation, enlightenment, and civili-

zation of the races. Not Wilberforce, Clarkson, Buxton, Lincoln, or "Uncle Tom's Cabin," have done more for the slave than David Livingstone. He seems to have possessed also an extraordinary power of sympathizing with and personally influencing the natives, with whom he came in contact.

This is a man of the old heroic type : a grand personality, like those of Xavier, Mazzini, Garibaldi, Bellot, Ross, Parry, Franklin, Stephenson, Watt, Mungo Park ; who exhibits, in a peculiarly fascinating phase of modern life, the heroic energy, and skilful perseverance in combating gigantic difficulties ; partly from ideal and humane ends— to serve God and Man—partly for the mere sake of combating those difficulties themselves. God is not tired of choosing and providing such natures, when He has a great work for them to do : indeed He provides also many obscurer workers, with natures as noble, whom He in His own way rewards. Are not men like Henry Martyn, and Bishop Patteson ; with other men and women, whose names remain hidden from the world; members of this heroic army ? Do we indeed lack heroes ?

In Canto VI. I relate the relief of Livingstone by Stanley; in Canto VII. Livingstone's death; and the wonderful transport of his remains by faithful followers, to the everlasting honour of a despised race ; finally, his honoured funeral in the grand cathedral of his own land. It remains that I express my obligations to the works of great African travellers — Speke and Grant, Baker, Burton, Schweinfurth, Du Chaillu, Winwood Reade, Moffatt, Stanley, Bowdich, Petherick— and to the correspondents of daily papers, who described the funeral.

UR tuneful students, with dull downward
      eyes,
Measuring one another in a dream,
Lisp, "how the pigmy time degenerates !
"Where are your 'heroes ? ' we distinguish none :
"Your 'heroes' have no literary style !
"Lo ! we discern some dust upon their feet."
They, poring on impalpable pale shades
Of vanish'd years, fantastically warble,
Singing sweet songs of phantoms in a cloud !
Delicate warblers, fleeting as a cloud !

    I lay my wreath upon a hero's grave.
There let it bloom ; or let it wither there !

LIVINGSTONE IN AFRICA.

CANTO I.

HE sun is sinking over Africa;
And under shadowy native eaves
    reclines
        A traveller upon a fur-strewn floor;
One whom no years' ignoble rust, but high
And holy toil have wasted; bearded grey,
In wayworn English garb he seems array'd;
His shoulders bow'd as from a life's long burden;
His rude wan countenance profoundly scarr'd
With noble ruin wrought by Love and Sorrow.
Reclined against the dwelling's claybuilt wall,
His falcon eyes explore the moonèd East.

Athwart a wondrous land that lies before
Slow shadow steals; o'er all the fervid palms,
Broadleaved banana, leaf-seas infinite,
Hoar unfamiliar stupendous forms
Of that primæval forest African:
Slowly the shadow with declining day
Fades rainbow splendour of the forest far,
And drowns imperial purple of the hills
In one phantasmal all-confounding gloom.

Ye mountains,[1] hiding undiscover'd worlds,
So mused in spirit the lone wanderer,
I hunger till I pass your mighty doors,
And lay my hand upon the Mystery!
African Andes, vast, inviolate,
Crown'd with the cloud, robed round with sombre
        forest,
Whose virgin snow no human feet profane
Have swept, but only the wild eagle's wing,
Of old your ghost on Rumour's shadowy breath
Wander'd abroad, O Mountains of the Moon!
And still ye are no more than a dim name:

Of old the Egyptian from your loins, that loom
Large in far realms of Rumour, drew the Nile.
Ye, couchant o'er the sultry continent,
Seem the great guardian Lion of Africa,
Who, from primæval ages all alone,
Silently stern, confronts a crimson dawn
Over fair Indian seas, with face that towers
Sunward, supreme; feeling a warm moist breath,
Faint with perfume, turn crystals of soft snow
Among the terrors of his icy mane;
Or, where the stature of his giant frame
Declines to westward, feeling the breath change
To rain within the hollows of his heart.
All, thundering down abrupt convulsed ravines,
Scarr'd in precipitous rugged flanks of stone,
Feed wide Nyanzas; whether there be twain,
Or many waters, these engender thee,
Wonderful Nile!
                        And yet I deem that I
Shall find thy parent springs remoter still.
Lualaba, with his tributary rivers,
And lilied lakes his loving bounty fills!

Yea, some have told me, and I well believe,
There are four fountains clear and deep as
    day,
Welling unfathomable, perennial
Among low hills as yet unseen, the last
Subsiding roll, it may be, of one range
Named of old Rumour, Mountains of the Moon.
Behold the shrine of living waters ! Here
From one immense rock-temple stream the Souls
Of many lands and nations, whispering
In dim enchanted caverns ; East and North,
And West emerging, sunny wings unfold :
Shouting they plunge in joyous waterfalls,
To roll a priceless silver all abroad,
Each to his Ocean, whose illustrious names
Are Congo, Nile, and long Leeambayee !
Whom Mother Ocean, in her awful arms
Absorbing, ever engendereth anew,
Gendering a holy Cycle evermore.

When royal Sun his Oriental bride,
India's Ocean, fiercely fervent woos,

While She dissolves in his delightful love,
What time He fronts earth's equatorial zone
On his way North to Cancer, then the waters
Rise in a tide of life upon the lands,
Lying athirst and barren in his blaze.

. . . . . My soul, unbow'd in face of failing years,
Though Hope may falter from unwearying
Hindrance of blind baseborn vicissitude,
Swears to resolve the alluring Mystery,
At whose cold feet our mightiest have fallen,
Yearning to find the sacred Source, and die ;
Nor have prevail'd; but if the Lord allow,
I and my fellow-labourers will prevail !

I seek the birth of that immortal River,
Who bears great Egypt in her watery womb,
Who nursed the world's prime empire on her
       bosom ;
And Moses, more illustrious than all
Pharoahs, her earth-enthralling conquerors,
Throned in their golden hundred-gated Thebes,

Tomb'd in hoar wonder of the pyramids.
At thy most holy source, primæval Nile !
The Greek drank wisdom ; yea, in solemn halls
Of Memphis, in columnar stone forests
Of mighty Karnac, rich with hieroglyph,
And pictured symbol and weird shapes of Gods.
Only the solar beam, the Obelisk,
Now from green palms and verdure and pure rills,
As then from sacred fountains of the Sun,
In olden time, in Heliopolis,
Still points with mystic granite flame to Heaven !
This mighty gnomon of a sun-dial
Moved then a shadow, lengthening among signs
Upon a porphyry or a brazen floor,
Among blithe forms of Pharaonic time ;
Now o'er young corn and red anemone !
There came Pythagoras to learn the lore
Of stars, and suns, and gods, and human souls ;
There Moses mused, well-nourish'd on rich stores
Of priests and sages ; communing with truth,
And in his spirit sifting dust from gold.
Only this one most ancient monument

Stands of thy glory, Heliopolis !
Earliest seat of learning, where the seer,
Illustrious Plato, came from Academe,
And sweet Ilissus ; fairest star of all
The fair young band who follow'd one wise
    master.
Here a stone astrolabe explored the night,
Measuring solemn wanderings of stars.
Here laboratory furnaces were glowing ;
While some astrologer with mystic rites
Drew horoscopes, or cast nativities :
But then our Earth, who in her equable
And proud obeisant motion round the sun
Hath in twice ten millennial periods
Her inclined axle measurably perturb'd,
Lean'd otherwise her pole among the skies ;
Another Polestar ruled the mariner ;
Another Ocean shrined thy radiance,
O Christian constellation of the Cross !
While otherwhere in every tranquil night,
Among cool calm abysses of pure space,
Shone Sirius, Arcturus, and Orion.

Here too the holiest Child of mortal race
Rested in humble guise with a pure Mother.

At thy most holy source, primæval Nile !
The Greek drank wisdom; learn'd a Dædal art,
That in his pure white light of genius,
In that pellucid æther of his clime,
Among pure breezes of Castalian hills,
And delicate unrobed consummate forms
Of radiant heroes, bloom'd in glorious
Marble immortal gods for all the world.

Here he beheld the blazon'd Zodiac
On loftiest firmaments of broad hewn stone
Within dim fanes, or solemn tombs of kings ;
Stupendous vaulted chambers in the heart
Of flame-hued mountain, silently aware
With populous imagery of men and gods,
Hawk or ram-headed; on wide wall and ceiling
Beheld a constellate celestial river
Meandering around a crystal sphere,
And navigated in twelve lives of Moons

By that resplendent Father of the Kings;
Kings lying here in glory, all embalm'd,
And jewell'd o'er with slumbering talismans,
Asleep in their immense sarcophagi.

Yonder, on burning sands of Libya,
Unmoved the tranquil-featured Sphinx beheld
Abraham, Homer, Solon, all the wise
Of every clime, who came, and saw, and wonder'd;
Who pass'd, leaving a heritage to man;
Beheld dissolving dynasties of Kings,
And all their people, pageant-like unroll'd
Before His face; they, with o'erwhelming pillars
Of desert sand before the whirlwind's breath,
Pass'd in loud pomp, and were not any more;
The silent Sphinx regarding, as to-day,
Beyond them all, serene Eternity!

There that colossal Memnon, while the Nile
Pour'd like another morning all around
Sweet life-engendering waters musical,
Murmur'd melodious salutation,

When first Aurora, his celestial mother,
Smiled sweet upon him from the Orient.

Fresh from fierce thunder of the cataracts,
Tortured among dark demon-blocks of stone
Fireborn, divine Nile smoothes his ruffled flow ;
Lingers a tranquil, a celestial lake
To embrace fair Philæ, Philæ, fairest isle
Of all earth's islands! fringed with mirror'd palm,
And lotos blossom on the crystalline
Laving her bosom ; she hath lotos blossom
For capitals of her hypæthral fane,
Quiet in heaven, tremulous in the river :
Where, sundering flowing phantoms of the stars,
Boats glide by night, aslant on broider'd sail,
Freighted with youth, and love and loveliness :
Balmy night breezes, all alive with song,
Laughter, and rhythmic plashing of light oars,
(While coloured lamp-lights lambent on the ripple
Stream from fair vessel, or embower'd shore) ;
Rustle tall fountain'd palms among the stars ;
As strange slim forms of a most ancient age

Land on pale quays of that so stately temple,
Sonorous with a gorgeous ritual.—
Now on a roofless column builds the stork!
Here, they believe, slumbers a mighty god,
Osiris, Love incarnate, and the Judge;
Also the Solar orb, and sacred Nile;
Who, with moon'd Isis and her little child,
Shadoweth forth a triune Deity.
His awful name none dare to breathe aloud:
An oath avails to bind for evermore
One who hath sworn "by Him that sleeps in Philæ."

Most ancient realm of all this ancient earth,[2]
Thought faints to sound thine hoar antiquity!
Europe and Asia were not when thy form
Brooded in solemn grandeur, as to-day,
Over dark ocean! when Dicynodon,
Ancestor of thy huge Leviathan,
Ruled over mightier seas and estuaries;
When melancholy vapours veil'd strange stars,
Ere man's wan yearning unavailing eyes
Awoke to wonder! ere the cataclysm

Rent all thy rocks, and summon'd forth the
    rivers . .
. . When came the Negro ?—and the dwindling
    Dwarf ?
I have found bones of immemorial age:
Their living families surround me now !

   Wilds more unknown than yonder ghostly Moon,
Beyond the bounds of Earth ! whose ruin huge
Of awful mountain, Albategnius,
Or Döerfel, whose abysses of dead gloom
Herschel in his enchanter's glass reveal'd !

   Africa ! vast immeasurable Void,
Where no imperial march of History
Solemn resounds from echoing age to age !
Haunt of light-headed fable and dim dream !
To whose fierce strand the Heaven-shadowing
    bird,
Enormous Roc, long deemed a wild romance,
Was wont to fly of old from Madagascar !—
In whose blue seas floats fragrant ambergris ;

Whose shores are blushing corallines most rare,
Where ocean-fairies wander mailed in gems,
Silently gliding through the branching bowers
While far inland strange palaces are piled
Profusely with pure ivory and gold—[3]
No lynx-eyed peril-affronting pioneer,
Since the beginning, until yesterday,
Dared violate thy sultry somnolence,
Couch'd, a grim lion in thine ancient lair ;
Sullenly self-involved, impenetrable !
Or if one ever bearded and aroused,
Thy winds have spurn'd his unrevealing dust !
Yea, in thy fiery deserts, in the pomp
Of lurid evenings, crimson, warm, like blood,
Thou dost devour thine own dark children,
    crouch'd
About thy cruel knees, dark Africa !

CANTO II.

ET mine are higher, holier purposes;
For I will cleave this darkling
  continent,
    As with a sword of intellectual light;
Lead these lost children to a living Father,
And tell them of a Brother who has died.
Yea, if my nature's weakness have rebell'd
Against what seems the world's indifference;
Men treading their unarduous wonted round
Of common care, oblivious of mine,
Who battle alone, afar from all; who waste,
Ignobly sinking here in sight of goal,
For bitter need of help I hoped from men,
At leisure in their calm abounding homes;
Bales for exchange or tribute; healing herbs;
Wherewith to calm this fire within my veins,
And tame the ravening hungry heathendom—

Thou knowest, O Lord, my prime solicitude
Was for the work Thou hast to me unworthy
Confided in Thy Providence unachieved,—
And yet I know the Holiest never fails
For lack of service ; but allows to each
The measure He in wisdom hath ordain'd.

For all the land is foul with monstrous wrong,
And desolation of the sons of Hell.
Surely the long long wail of human woe
Ever ascends from all our earth to heaven !
But here the mist of blind unending tears
Hangs undissolving, and abolishes
Yon very Life-Light from His shining halls,
And hides the Father from his orphan'd sons.
Hell is let loose ; and jubilant cruelty
Tortures a feeble lowly-witted race,
Poor fallen outcast of humanity ;
Inflames the lurking salvage brute that haunts
A wilding blood to fratricidal war,
To thrall its very kindred, for the sport
Of paler large-brain'd fiends, the common foe,

And glut their markets with the flesh of men.
Shoot them and drown them! from convulsive arms
Tear small sweet clinging babes, and fainting brides
From lovers, who with unavailing life
Stain them in falling, or themselves enslaved,
Yoked, goaded, pinioned, tramp the burning wilds,
To bleach with beast-gnawn bones the wilderness ;
Or huddled in a slaver's pestilent hold,
Writhing and raving, rotting while alive,
Are flung to gorge sleek monsters of the sea !
Lo ! in dusk offings of ensanguined seas,
At sunset doth the torpid slaver droop
Her guilty sail ; while evil strangers brand
Dark women on a golden strand with fire ;
Who are mute with endless woes unutterable !
    Nay ! the long wail of wounded innocence
Hath ne'er been squander'd on a voiceless Void !
But every tear of every helpless child
Sinks in a warm unfathomable Love :
And armèd Righteousness awaits her hour,
Albeit Her lightning slumber in the cloud.
These human shambles shall be purged from blood :

This charnel of the world shall reek no more,
Plague-spot of all the starry universe !
For I will flash the light of Europe's eyes
Full on the tyrant, till he quail and cower,
And vanish, a mere snowflake in the sun.
England, inviolate Ark of Freedom, launch
Thy thunder as of old ; and hurl them low !
Fulfil thy mission ! fallen heroes want
Yonder in heaven their crown of blessedness,
Till the last bondsman clasp unfetter'd hands
O'er the last slaver, whelm'd beneath the wave !

But I abide until my task be done.
And if they slay their mortal enemy,
It is the Lord who calls, and it is well—
When they had thought to murder ; reft from me
All I most cherish'd on a former day ;
Killing my converts, even the little ones,
Or sweeping them into captivity ;
I said, " I am not less resolved than they :
They do but save me wills and codicils ! "
I turn my face indeed, as they intend,

C

From this my labour of long years o'erthrown ;
And yet not homeward, baffled as they deem—
For lo ! my face is toward the world unknown,
That seem'd almost the very world in sooth,
" From whose dark bourne no traveller returns."
I take the plunge, and I am lost in night !
Lost to the life and tumult of mankind :
No voice may reach me from the homes of men ;
No voice of mine may penetrate to them.
Five times twelve moons have filled their horns
          and waned ;
My memory is failing from the world ;
Only a ghostly rumour murmurs low
How one has seen a strange white wanderer,
Somewhere inland ; none certainly knows where ;
And one more rumour whispers, he is dead.
Empires may rise and fall ; great wars may
          thunder ;
And peace may follow war ; and I not know,
More than the drown'd who slumber in the sea—
Yea, have they ruin'd me at Kolobeng ?
Behold I wrest from them all Africa !

For I will never cease from journeying,
Until the length and breadth of all the land
Shine forth illuminate from shore to shore !
My life is one long journey ; and I love
Peril, and toil, and strange vicissitude ;
Exploring all the wonder of the world
On sea and land ; wonder for evermore ;
And all the marvellous miracle of man.
I am urged ever by a restless ghost,
And may not fold my hands in tranquil sleep.
Yet when we have grown old, we want the glow
Of our own generous children in their prime,
Warming our twilight ; they love thought for us,
As we of old for them ; their little ones
Play, like a dear last dawn, around our age ;
And I too long to be at home again
By the sweet firelight of my northern land !
At Christmas-time, the room is bright with green,
And far bells faintly peal athwart the snow :
Then quiet firelight, wavering with soft sound,
Pleasantly ruddies gold and silver hair :
But in the summer, little children sing

Anear a shimmer of slim aspen leaves,
Fluttering with sound of summer rain.
Ah ! shall I never cease from journeying ?
Urged ever onward by a restless ghost,
I may not fold my hands in pleasant sleep !

When I surmount some unfamiliar height,
Behold ! an alien realm mysterious
Unroll'd in twilight ! ghostly, drear, and wan ;
Stain'd with what seem huge bombs of shatter'd
          iron,
Hurl'd from a weird infernal enginery.
And then I muse what eerie living things
Dwell far beyond among the mists of night—
Whether the wanderer may wander on
For ever in the waste, hearing no sound,
Save of his own footfall ; or yonder dwell.
Dark unimaginable human lives ;
Wearing what uncouth forms, allied to some
Misshapen horrors of the forest wild—
Weird startling mockery of immortal man ;
Shocking the soul with chill mistrustful fear,

And doubt of her pre-eminent destiny—
Brutebrow'd, brutemaw'd, huge hirsute prodigies,
Challenging with a vast appalling roar
Whoso disturbs their monstrous monarchy !
Dark unimaginable human lives,
Ever alone in this most ancient realm,
Immured in a stupendous sepulchre,
Afar from man's tumultuous chariot-race
Of sounding splendour ; somnolent aware
How the dull tide of dim inglorious years
Moves ever foul and lurid with the scurf
Of ruin'd blood, and gold, and scalding tears !

Some veer small restless, rambling, apelike eyes ;
Their clicking gibber mimics flittermice ;
A skeleton people plucking roots and berries
For starved subsistence, grubbing shallow holes,
Or sheltering in borrow'd dens disused.   .   .   .
What people lies before me ? some affirm
That there be men sepulchred verily
In subterranean chambers like the dead ;
Burrowing human moles, fleeing from light,

By their free choice, and immemorial
Usage ; though Rumour murmurs her wild tale
Ever with a light head confusedly.

Shall I behold some dark terrific cave,
Reeking with bats, and owls, and doleful things,
High among crags of a precipitous mountain,
Strewn with fresh bones of men, that hideous ghouls
In human form, foul anthropophagi,
Have gnawn for food ; a loathsome den defiled
With dripping human members, torn for meat ?
A desolate wind howls ever dolefully
Around the dismal open mouth of hell,
Howls like a murdered man's avenging soul !
While among boulder-ruins of the mountain
Climb beasts obscene, scenting a horrid feast !
At night a thunder of great lions rolls,
Rebellowing from basalt precipices :
At night a fervour of infernal flame,
With cruel yells of hellish revelry,
Affronts pale stars ; what time the unearthly fiends
Grimy, and gash'd with knives, and foul with earth,

Squat mumbling bodies of lost travellers,
Whom they decoying fell'd with monstrous
    clubs.
But underneath the floor of their black vault
Deepens a hollow murmur, far withdrawn
Within the haunted heart of the dread mountain.
It may be mutter'd wrath of slumbering fires;
It may be secret waters wandering;
But they believe it of another world;
And shuddering pour libation to the god.

Sometimes by night a mightier thunder even
Than thunder of roaring lions, like an ocean,
Bursts all the boundaries of ruinous heaven
In one wild flood of universal flame,
With sound as of upheaval of adamant;
Towering wrath of Powers immeasurable,
And roll'd war-chariots of tremendous cloud:
Sound the great mountains in their chasms and
    craters,
Bastions, and inviolable towers,
Rebellow; hurl abroad; mutter in gloom;

Brood over in their dim and sullen souls.
Perpetual seas of broad purpureal flame,
With intervals of momentary night,
Dark as the darkness of a man born blind,
Possess the sky's unfathomable concave;
Wherein appalling growths of more intense
Fire with seven branches, like gigantic trees,
Spring up and vanish ! . . . .
Behold yon perpendicular crags, like flame,
Whose melaphyre and porphyry condor crests
Threaten the valleys ! whose profound ravines
Of deadly twilight ne'er a sun may see,
Unsoften'd of a tiniest herb or flower !
Now furious torrents toss white manes of foam
Down their long solitudes ; the firmament
Sunders, and pours dense watery deluges,
Illuminate with deluges of light ;
Howls the tornado ; 'tis the reign of chaos !
Great lions lashing tails in grim despair,
Mingling their roar with elemental thunder,
Climb from   the   floods, or   struggling drown
        therein !

Ah ! would the blinding falchion of swift light-
  ning,
That crimson wounds the mountain flank, but hurl
One of those loosen'd bounding blocks of rock,
So as to stop for ever the black mouth
Of that infernal cavern of the fiends,
Where still a madden'd laughter peals among
Commotions of Divine wrath flying abroad,
Reiterate from all their haunted halls !
Lo ! the tornado, and the levinbolt
Have fallen upon yon tree's enormous bulk,
Hard by the cave ; blasting, and wrenching it
Loose from a cleft it grappled for centuries
With serpentine huge roots! it creaks and crashes !
Headlong it topples to the gulf that boils !

Some even tell a marvellous dim tale
Of a tribe buried somewhere in the wild ;
A satyr-race of clovenfooted men,
Hairy and tail'd, with cloven feet like swine !
Where are the Pigmies ?   Homer sang of old
Their yearly war with southward-flying cranes !

They wear enormous heads upon their shoulders
They build their pigmy booths in dim recesses
Of some impenetrable forest world !
Two travellers [4] lately came upon their traces.

Here are no mouldering monuments of glory,
Confused dim ruin of long centuries ;
As though ashamed of human purposes,
Suffering slow conversion to the ways
Of soft-outlined harmonious natural things,
Flower and herb, and weatherhued worn stone.
Yet here Napoleons and Tamerlanes
Have temper'd to a life-devouring sword
The drossy coarseness of humanity :
Only their mighty Mother in more scorn
Spurns in an hour the poor fantastic toil !
A millstone, lost in verdure or black ooze ;
Cairns upon hillsides ; fragments of rude jars ;
Obsidian implements with fossil bones,
Buried in bowels of unquarried rock ;
These are the memories Earth retains of man.
And yet the dead are in the forest mould,

In branching wildernesses of rich gloom,
In beast, and bird, and every living thing;
Yea, noble thoughts and deeds and souls for ever
Live in the deep eternal heart of God :
They are reverberate in the lives of all;
Nor fail of full fruition and reward.[5]

Or shall I light on some barbarian
Court, where high lords, like reptiles in the dust,
Grovel before a swarthy emperor,
Throned all in gold? who—from the burning day
Shielded beneath a slave-supported silk
Pavilion crown'd with some griffonian beast,
That courts the sunlight—clothed in musky fur
Of tawny spotted pard, cruel as he,
And fig-bark beaten; wrists with ivory bound,
And slung with genets' tails; a scimitar
In his right hand ; red plumes of touraco [6]
Among his oil'd elaborated curls—
Glowers where the panther-supple guards advance,
Gory, dusk, jewell'd stalwart Amazons,
At his feet rolling four distorted heads.

Three skulls of kings, late mighty mortal foes,
The monarch tramples ; a white ivory trump
Of elephant tusk one blows, while others clang
Dissonant gongs—but ah ! delicious groves
Of fanlike palm, with waxen clusters fair,
Cassia, myrrh, aloe, or ananas !
Sweet amber-weeping mists of sensitive leaf,
Wooing young sunlight to a delicate
Dream in your soft warm zephyr-haunted hearts,
Empetall'd all with rosy peach blossom !
Alas ! your mellow meeklived innocence
Blazes—A fierce intolerable gold
Breaks from breastplates of yelling murderers,
Dragging men, women, children, cowering slaves,
From hence, and shelter of dank cane jungles,
Or wounding chaos of floral parasite ;
Convolved wing'd serpents hung in gorgeous gloom
Of tower-pillar'd forest high and hoar.
Rather they brave grim Terrors of the wild,
Stealthily prowling in moonlighted glades,
Where bubble sweet live waters musical ;
Huge grisly rivals crushing the stunn'd prey ;

Than surerfooted more unerring doom
Of hate fraternal, or implacable
Unholy violence of holy men,
Who, glutting a false god's bloodthirstiness,
Hale them, poor innocents, to sacrifice !
A king hath died ; and all dead emperors
They worship with lewd rites of cruelty,
By " watering " malignant evil dust
With what in its malignant vampire life
A vain, unstable, sanguinary soul
Relish'd to quaff from a foe's hollow skull,
More than all nectar—crimson human blood.
Yea, all the forest is one Golgotha ;
Skeletons, skulls, and cumbering carcases,
Confused in one delirious dread dream !
Behold ! under yon ancient fetish tree,
Defiled with slaughter of five centuries,
Near an uncouth hewn stone (a phallic idol,
Begrimed, and hung with ghastly offerings)
A human victim horribly tormented !
One blade thrust like a bit between his jaws
Is strain'd and fasten'd there ; while many knives

Lacerate all his gory frame ; he writhes
In agony ; for every living wound
Men have inflamed with diabolic art !

A pomp barbarian reigneth everywhere.
Nobles are slung in hammocks of rich silk,
Turban'd, and motley'd with quaint ornament ;
Or rest their gold-encumber'd arms on heads
Of young lithe favourites, wearing cloth of gold ;
Velvety smooth boys, eyed with slumbrous fire ;
While others flirt long gold-bound elephant-tails.
Nigh to the monarch squats a hideous dwarf ;
And a white negro with two small pink eyes.
There is a trampling of arm'd cavalry ;
Barbs in rich mail, brightly caparison'd,
Mounted by swarthy horsemen, champ the bit,
Their riders quivering bronze assegais.
Hearken ! lewd revelry of dancing slaves,
Clashing with cymbal, tabor, castanet. . .

CANTO III.

OW in my far enchanted solitude,
My long life moves before me like a
dream . . .

A child in Ulva, by the Northern sea,
I hear my father at our evening prayer,
And wild Gael singing of my grandmother.
A factory boy upon the banks of Clyde;
For all the dissonant whirl of enginery,
I seize the food of learning, swiftly glancing
On some dear volume, laid upon a marge
Of the great spinning-jenny, as I pass,
Repassing ever in monotonous toil.
Fired with the splendour of the Lord of Love,
I long to unfurl His standard in the world:
For this I conquer arts laborious
Of serviceable healing; and I grow
Adept in many a helpful handicraft;

So full equipp'd, with arduous effort arm'd,
Living a temperate, reasonable life,
I bear a stout heart in a season'd frame ;
And emulous of illustrious pioneers,
Nor all unmindful of my sires austere,
I find myself i' the heart of Africa,
Helping the father of my bride to be.

My long life moves before me like a dream.
Behold ! our mission-house at Kolobeng :
These labour-roughen'd hands have builded it.
Nor for myself alone, but for the dark
Children of whom I am the father here,
I labour with strong hand, and heart, and soul.
I smelt rude ores ; and, fervid as large eyes
Of wrathful tigers, ringing iron yields
Upon mine anvil, hammer'd heartily ;
While a bow'd native plies the goatskin bellows.
Lusty and hale, in manhood's vigorous prime,
I startle the lone woods with stalwart blows ;
While cream-white splinters fly from stubborn
        trunks,

Whose leafy pride falls headlong shattering ;
My wife with finger nimble, dexterous,
Moulding the while a hundred things at home.

There is a power enthralling human souls
In equal dealings, in a lofty life,
And lowly Love's unwearying ministry.
One who inherits wisdom's treasure-house,
And lives endow'd with more than wonted grace
Of human faculty, may forge the gold
Thereof to ignominious chains for men ;
Or twine the spiritual wealth, for their
Deliverance, to cords of fair persuasion,
Wooing their own endeavours after God.
I wielding for the common use, not mine,
A wider knowledge and a riper skill,
Bestow'd free counsel or sincere reproof ;
Tended my children when their bodies ail'd ;
Lent a large heart to small perplexities,
And simple tales of hourly human woe. . . .
. . . Have these a lowlier place allotted them ?
Yet they full surely have their post prepared

D

In God's world-army : I will help them there.
And I believe Jesus, the Man of men,
Who is God's personal Love and Righteousness,
To be the one and only living Lord,
Ruler alike of loftiest and least,
Who, being reveal'd, will draw men unto Him,
Each in his order and foreknown degree.

Sun of the living ! Hesper of the gloom !
Surely Thy dusky children call for Thee,
Unknowing whom they call—the wail resounds
Yet in mine ears of some funereal dirge
For one beloved and vanish'd ; when the moon
Wavers, as if in water, among leaves
Of air-moved umbrage ; and a bark-built village
Lies in pale elf-light, with embowering palm
And silvern plantain ; lonely forest shades
Of over-frowning mountain-presences
With stealthily mysterious forms aware.
A bitter, long, monotonous human wail !
More poignant than the cries of animal lives
In unreverberate torture ; 'tis a wail

Of one that's cloven to the depths of being,
Maim'd in the vitals of an immortal soul.
To me it seems alive with the wild prayer,
This poor blind people hath so oft preferr'd,
Crying with dumb yet infinite eloquence,
" O wise white man ! we pray thee give us sleep!"
So moans a hollow voice reverberate
In long-drawn aisles of some sepulchral vault;
So moans the mystic growth Mandragora,
Feeding on human ravage in a ruin
Under a gibbet, when one pulls the root.
How long have these then cower'd here in night,
Mouthpieces of creation's misery,
Wailing the world's wail in closed ears of God ?
Whom now lament they ? some beloved friend,
Chief, mother, bride, or child, who turn'd so
        cold
And strange and silent; who may not abide
Any more here in sweet sunlight with them,
Or pleasant interchange of word and smile ;
Gone forth for ever from them to the chill
And cheerless realm of dreams impalpable

Nevermore ! wails the burden of the strain,
Burdening, as it seems, the very sleep
Of a serene, fair incense-breathing earth !
Ever it wails, low, dreary, and desolate,
Oppress'd and muffled in a solemn sorrow ;
A dirge world-weary, an old-world requiem,
Trailing a slow wan length along the dust,
Faint from the fount of immemorial tears ;
A shadow, whose maim'd wings are plumed with
        awe ;
Sunken so deep from ghostly woes and fears,
And broken hearts of all ancestral lives ;
Phantoms aroused by a fresh living pain
To haunt the labyrinths of a living soul,
And all the dark slow movement of the dirge !

One cabin stands a little way apart
From all the rest upon a higher ground.
Hence flows the wail ! A man laments his son.
It is an aged warrior of the tribe,
Who cowers, and sways himself upon the floor,
Before an ember glow, that he beholds

Only in dreaming ; while a warm, red gleam
Falls on the brown of rude encircling wall,
Leaving a smoke-beclouded roof in gloom ;
Falls on barb'd javelins, and bows and arrows,
And many hunting spoils of him who lies
Near to his father, silent, stark, and cold ;
Ruddies the dark bare limbs of life and death.
Rich furs are under and over the young form ;
Furs golden, furs of lynx, and ocelot :
A small uncomely dog, with pointed ears,
Presses his faithful body to the corpse.
He was a comely boy, a mighty hunter,
A bold young warrior, hope of all the tribe,
And his infirm old father's only stay.
When humid morning, chill, and pale, and wan,
Peers at those intervals between the boughs
Of wattled wall, yon ashes will be grey,
And still the old man be cowering by the dead !
Then the fond faltering sire must wander forth
Alone ; away from this unpitying herd
Of yet unwounded men into the wild ;
There to fade slowly ; with a feeble hand

Plucking the berries, pulling up the roots ;
A living skeleton, grim woe and want
In dim, scared eyes ; until the wolf and raven
Find him low laid, their unresisting prey !

The father's wail, like mournful waves unseen,
Dies on the ear, and moans alternately ;
But later, figures gather in the open,
Lamenting by a fire new-made the dead. . . .
What wizard, with his incantation curst,
Blasted the living ; changing to a foe,
And chilling fear, what was so amiable ? [7]
Over the shoulder timorously glance
They, at the very rustling of a leaf,
To where the dead lie yonder in the forest,
Strewn with some humble offerings they need :
Food, bowls, or ivory, arms, and hunting gear.
Now beat loud tamtams ; rattle hollow drums !
So scare away the dim unhomely ghost
With yells, and shouts, and drunken revelry. . . .
" Ah ! shadow-muffled panther, with fierce eyes,
Prowling and mumbling yonder, art thou he ?

Ah ! whispering leaves of darkling forest trees !
Ye are ill whispers of infernal fiends !
But we will drown the bitterness of woe,
Frowning, foreboding, and bewildering fear ! "

8 Behold ! one stalks emergent from a cave
In yon far-off enfoldings of the hills,
Where he has lain in some enchanted swoon,
From when the moon her slender silver bow
Lifted in blue night, till she rose an orb,
Fully resplendent argent, even now.
And he is haggard, worn, emaciate
With vigil and with fast; a tawny hide
Of some wild beast about his grimy frame,
Charms of link'd leopard's teeth upon his breast,
And leopard's liver for an amulet.
With stainèd, hideous face, and jingling bells,
And for a head-gear feathers of a bird,
He sits among the mourners by the fire.
Then all gesticulating chaunt a prayer ;
Till he, the prophet, fearfully convulsed,
Falls like a corpse ; but all the people cry :

"Oh moon ! Ilogo ! spirit of the moon !
Thine are the rivers,
        Thine, Ilogo !
And the wilds and mountains,
        Thine, Ilogo !
Reveal who hath enchanted our beloved !
Oh moon ! Ilogo ! spirit of the moon !
        Hear us, Ilogo !"

And then the prophet from his death-like swoon
Arouses ; from communion with the Moon.
His dusky tribe are gathering around ;
Silence falls ominous on all intent ;
Till with harsh, croaking tones the devil proclaims :
" Lamoli ! it was *she* bewitch'd the dead !"
Then all the naked savages roll eyes
Of fanatic fury, and, yelling horribly,
Rush   toward   a   leaf-thatched   cabin,   shouting
        hoarse :
"Let the Muave draught convict the witch !"
They drag from thence a shrieking, innocent maid,
Who shivers with the pang of mortal fear :

Hustled she drains among the cursing crew
Ordeal poison from a gourden bowl,
And, struggling piteous to reverse the doom
Of her young murder, reels, and sinks, and falls ;
A hundred daggers mangling her fair life. . . . .
Do these not need the Gospel of the Lord ?

Therefore I press right onward to my goal :
Nor only for an hour, a month, a year ;
But while life lasts, a warrior to the end,
I wrest from Fortune all she would withhold.
Even as a lion in his sultry lair
Shakes off a myriad dew-drops from his mane,
So have I spurn'd all hampering obstacle,
Regarding danger with a quiet smile.
O civilizer, shrink from Violence !
Use Righteousness, and broad Humanity,
With temperate firmness ; govern your own
        selves,
And so the people : yet never seem to fear ;
Nor be ye loth to call auxiliar might
Of muscular right arm, or deadly rifle,

If these prove helpful in extremity.

Whose guiltless blood weighs on my soul to-day?
I have not injured, mock'd, insulted any:
I have been wanting in an English pride;
Nor feel the grand immeasurable gulf,
Which every drunken subaltern may feel
Between the veriest scum of England's isle,
And of all infusorial "foreigners"
The least unworthy—nay; for even him,
Whom, with all colour'd races of the world,
We from superior panoramic heights,
With one judicial and exhaustive wave
Of hand, may name and sweep from sympathy,
Even the "*damn'd nigger*" I have not contemn'd;
Knowing that if the Lord regarded us
Proud English from "damn'd nigger" points of
          view,
All would be damn'd indeed without reprieve.

⁹ A lion once, a mightiest male lion,
Whom my good rifle's bullet had but maim'd,

Sprang in his wrath; one huge and ponderous paw,
Striking my shoulder, hurl'd me under him.
Over me stood the vast dilated beast
Growling; his paw weigh'd on my shatter'd
      shoulder;
His great eyes glower'd; his fangs gleam'd terrible;
Like a simoom, his breathing scorch'd my face;
With tawny wilderness of mane aroused,
Frowning, aloft he swung his tufted tail.
But God removed all terrors and all pain:
When the brute shook me, numb indifference
Stole over all my being, while I watch'd;
Yea, look'd into the formidable eyes!
(So Love tempers inevitable blows
Of Fate for all the sons of suffering:)
A comrade fires; the lion springs on him;
Then fainting staggers,—ponderous falls—and dies.

My long life moves before me like a dream.

We fell'd our way through groves impervious
To healthful daylight; realms of ravenous beast,

And venom'd snake secreted in the gloom ;
Dismal dead trees enshrouded with the pale
Dense life of lichen that hath stifled them ;
Where lurks foul carrion, and agarics
Fouler than carrion infect the air,
Mid noisome immemorial forest mould.
We crush'd through deadlier thickets of rank
      growth,
Whose blades colossal, notch'd with tearing teeth,
Rise in dense walls above the ox-rider :
These wound, entangle : while his lower limbs
Are chill'd by shadowy dews that ne'er exhale
From labyrinths of marshlight-haunted fen,
Dismal in dull death-gendering decay,   .
His head and shoulders burn with torrid fire,
Unshelter'd from a humid sultry sky.
My body and my raiment rent with thorns,
These lacerated feet refuse to bear
Me any further ; and I linger long,
A prisoner, waiting for my wounds to heal.
I have waded waist-deep in stagnating water
Of inundated equatorial plains,

And, swathed in saturated raiment, march'd
On, till hot air hath drain'd their moisture dry;
Then, for how many torturing nights and days
Have I lain in the gripe of dire disease,
Clinging inveterate to devour my life;
Evil inharmonious monsters ravening
Around these hells of my delirium!
When poor dark savage brothers tended me
With a white wife's untiring tenderness.
Some hearts, in sooth, of those my followers,
Quailing before long toil herculean,
Weary of peril in the very air
We breathe, a Protean never-sleeping peril,
Often immeasurable, unforeknown,
Shrank from my side; yea, even some of whom
I had hoped better things—but some, alas!
Were weak and worthless instruments, that break
In hands of whoso trusts in a fair show:
And some were agents of the slave-trader,
Sworn to oppose, and drive me to despair.

Anon we travel

Over immense brown regions, no sweet rain
Rendereth mild with gracious influence :
A harsh rude waste, hated by man and beast ;
Where the foot sinks in scorching loose brown sand
At every toilsome footfall ; while the sun
Strikes upward from a powdery parch'd earth,
Tanning and blistering : fiercely from on high
He smites upon bow'd heads of travellers,
Under arch'd awning of a labouring wain,
Or swaying slowly on a lean worn ox.
Poor oxen ! how they pant, and loll the tongue,
Beaten of urgent teamsters with loud whips,
Pulling at wheels, that settle clogg'd with sand.
Shadows are sharply blotted on the ground :
Blue blazing daylight glares intolerable :
In a half-dreaming doze we journey on,
Still for our sole horizon the wan waste.
But when some watermelon loll'd before us,
How all rush'd eager on the priceless prize,
A large green ball upon an arid soil !
Slashing the cool pink pulp, that wells with life,
And burying mouths in fair fresh nectar-springs.

How terrible is thirst!
Days without water! ne'er a watermelon
Even, to slake a moment hell's own drought! . . .
Hark! shouts of joy break in upon the drear
Faint slumbrous silence of our fiery way:
All startled raise dim half-closed aching eyes—-
Behold the lake! our goal in sight! Hurrah!
Lofty palmyras, palm, acacia,
O'er hazy waters purple in the sun,
Who sets below in solitary glory—
And surely on a pale horizon line
Tall sable horsemen galloping furiously!
See the slow oxen gaze aroused, and lowing
Hasten—behold black bulks of elephant,
And slim giraffes, show water to be near!
Shall we pursue?

. . . They dwindle, waver, and change;
All blows like slanting flame; drifting divides.
It was the Satan's simulated water!
And only mist roll'd over a salt plain.
Yet the same region hath its wither'd herb;

Wells that fill slowly when one deftly digs ;
Stunted green bushes, pools of rainwater,
Where skeleton women drink from ostrich eggs ;
And even springs where tall lush grasses grow.
Here the light zebra, and the swift wild ass,
Bound by elastic, and the shaggy gnu
Glares with red eye ; here bristle porcupines ;
Fussy ichneumon scuttles ; ratels tumble ;
Ash-hued coarse-haired anteaters with long snout
Lurk, like distortions of a curious dream.

My long life moves before me like a dream !

The cheerful bustle of the morning march !
Shouts of the driver ; scuffling of loud beasts !
Delicious swims and baths in some lone pool,
With chestnut-colour'd leaves in the blue glass,
And gorgeous birds reflected as they fly !

Appears the dear wild nightly bivouac
In some dim forest,—I upon a couch
Of woven rushes, under a furr'd hide,

Shelter'd, it may be, by a roof of boughs.
A grimy cauldron slung athwart the blaze
Held our repast of savoury buffalo-meat:
(Ere sunset had my rifle slain the beast)
But now my dusky troop surround the fire,
That ruddies their swart forms and visages,
Leaping to flame, with crackling faggot piled;
Subsiding soon to embers deeply glowing.
Illumined smoke drifts fragrant, wavering
Among mazes of long involved llianas,
That seem in the red, hesitating light,
To move alive, like pythons watching prey.
There breathes a strange, delicious woodland smell;
Resinous amber glimmers to the stars;
Richly-dim blossoms, many-hued, immense,
Droop fragrant heaven, a milky way of flowers,
Wherein by day the nimble monkey hurries,
And gorgeous parrot screams—now all is hush'd.

Yet there are weird, wild songs about the fire
Peals of a reckless, frolic merriment,
Immoderate jests of nature's shameless child

E

Dazed with the wassail-bowl, and fumes that rise
From gurgling gourds, to steal bewilder'd sense,
Sense light as thistle-down ; gay young buffoons,
And elder fools allowing allusions free,
With frantic, half-lewd gestures, bounden only
By salutary fear of me, the Master . . . .

One tells a tale of perilous hunts with spear,
Envenom'd arrows, shields of rugged hide ;
Relates the infuriate, unwieldy charge
Of rough, one-horn'd, uncouth rhinoceros ;
Or elephant snapping crush'd dishevell'd trees,
With horrible, ear-bursting trumpet-bray.
They tell of graceful, lithe, long-neck'd giraffes,
Beating the plain with undulating flight ;
Strong striding ostrich, spurning the burnt sand ;
Of crawling dumb to leeward of a herd—
Kudu, or eland wearing wreathen horns.

Or they relate some wonderful weird tale
Of sorcery and superstition strange ;
For one affirms he knew in such a village

A man who turn'd at intervals to leopard,
Lurking in dens to feed upon mankind;
Anon the beast's heart gather'd strong within him;
Burn'd to devour, to lap the blood of men;
Until the lust of death beyond control
Drove him from home into the awful wild—
Where, horror! transformation swiftly grew
From the inhuman heart to the man's mind,
And human limbs—behold! he crouches low,
Fire-eyed, in act to spring—sleek, supple beast,
His body of flame starr'd over with black night:
Large-brain'd, blood-thirstiest of the infernal crew,
Six human victims hath the wizard slain,
Ere, man once more, the avengers torture him,
Avowing with bitter tears the sorcery. . . . .
Then many a negro, shivering, glances round,
Timidly peering into forest gloom;
They pile more wood; sitting in silence, till
Another adds his marvel to the store.

Is it all fable? is it all illusion?
Nay, doth not our most awful Universe

Lead poor, mad mortals to the wilds alone,
Into a barren wilderness of souls;
Mask'd in stern iron, prison'd in adamant,
A fiery gulf between them and the world;
Forbidden dear embracings of their kind,
And mutually yielding thoughts of all?
Though girt with kindly, once familiar faces,
Lonelier they than are the lonely dead;
Or haunted only by fell fiends that scowl
Out of the very eyes of sleepless love!
God whirls them forth, and sets them in a cleft
Of some ice-armour'd, cloud-robed precipice: ฺ
It snows, it howls; the everlasting mountains
Reel, crashing downward in the lightning's eye:
God murmurs in their ears a Mystery
In tongues unknown, of import terrible,
That none may hear or comprehend but they;
Nor even they, but in maim'd cadences;
Wind-wilder'd murmurs of a music wild.
Ah! we all wander blindly in a dream!
Save for a revelation from the Lord.

They tell of our adventures by the road,
Wonderful, fearful, laughable or grave;
Gesticulating passionately gay,
Grimacing with a monkey-mimicry.
One says that white men rise from the salt sea;
Verily live below the green water;
Whence comes our long, lank compromise for hair :
The water we inhabit straightens it!
They mention my rough dog, poor old Chitani,[10]
Whom they affirm I cherish for his tail,
A tail that curls to right and not to left;
A tail by learnèd men discredited!

My trusty followers, my Makololo,
Astound the rest, relating how they toil'd
Athwart the continent;[11] arriving last
On a subsiding ridge of table-land;
Whence without warning burst upon their view,
Ocean!
　　　　Vision never dream'd before—
On Him in His sublime infinitude,
Soliloquizing awful in the gloom;

With one intolerable rift of light
Vibrating in the immeasurable waste
Of massy, torn, wan water that ascends,
To meet confusion of the hurrying cloud,
Releasing misty momentary rays ;
While in this shifting gulf of utter light,
A snowy sail shows black as ebony.

" Spell-bound we pause : we had follow'd this
      our Father,
Him of the honest heart, our wise white friend,
Through weal and woe, a weary, weary way,
From our own homes ; in face of all the people
Spake, while we journey'd through their several
      lands,
That never white man brought an African
Here to the coast, save only to enslave ;
But we would trust our father ; we had proved
Him well, and he had promised ; yea, we know
The English have good hearts for Africa !
And yet we pause at the sublime surprise.
For we had faith in what our Ancients told,

That the great World continueth evermore ;

And now the World Himself saith unto us,

' Lo ! I am ended ! there is no more of me !'

Moreover, marching on with our sick Leader,

Whom we support, astounded we discern

Dwellings of white men, mountains of white stone

With caves therein ! and, yet more wonderful,

Upon the water, rolling near inshore,

A painted floating town, with fronting idol !

A giant bird with great white flapping wings,

Whose thunderous rebellion men that swarm

In windy, reeling heights are conquering

By strong enveloping of resolute arms !

Then, trusting to the word of our good Father,

Half timidly we climb the floating town,

Whose common soldiers, mariners, and chiefs

Pay joyful homage to our own dear lord ;

And all of them have kindly hearts for us.

But round the wooden walls dark, iron mouths

Of demons gape ; whence, being touch'd with fire,

Leap   thunderous   lightnings,   Genii   clothed   in

    smoke !

Pointing to them, our Father said to us,—
' With these grim mouths we stop the sale of men !'
And then our Father, very near to death,
Though his white friends would fain have borne
      him home,
Would suffer not his children to pursue
Alone their arduous perilous return :
' My Makololo boys have served me well,'
Said he, ' and I will not desert them now !'"

Well I remember, O my splendid Sea,
How thy salt breath blew o'er me, as alive !
After interminable deserts drear,
And dank hot jungles of the savage race,
To come upon thee, Ocean, unaware,
Dear native element of all the free !
With British tars, and British hearts of oak,
And the old fiery flag upon the wind !
Tears blind my vision—yonder England lies !
A grey gull, in his strong deliberate flight
Hover'd and slanted, dipp'd his breast in brine,
Exulting in the wind and turbulent foam ;

While half the mortal languor left my limbs,
And I rejoiced with him.   From sea to sea!
I traversed all the dark, blank continent;
And proved it not, as timid idle dream
Surmised, an evil waste unprofitable,
Huge blot on God's most bountiful, fair world;
Rather a promised land of living waters !
Like that king's daughter in the fairy tale,
Asleep, awaiting her Deliverer.

How clearly do mine inner eyes behold
The dear, wild nightly bivouac of yore,
When I was in my manhood's vigorous prime !
If it were in the prairie, or the desert,
Sinbad, my riding ox, with other oxen,
Would lie beside the looming bullock-wain,
Audibly ruminating, couch'd at ease
Upon his shadow, in a luminous moon.
If it were in a forest, such as last
Appear'd before my musing memory;
When I have heard awhile my followers' tales,
Wearily close mine ears in first faint sleep,

Half hearing only broken words, and names
Of tribes or places, weird, and all germane
To the mysterious realm of forest wild.
But later still, silence inviolate reigns ;
Save for a low communing of weird wind
Among high crowns of leafy ebonies,
Moving and murmuring, while star-worlds pass
    over.
When I awake, dark forms are lying round :
Firelight warms faintly mighty sylvan pillars,
Rising from gloom to gloom : they seem to my
Drowsed senses ancient phantoms of the night.
Thousands of years, some say, the huge Mowana
Flourishing lives, while mortal men around
Fall with his leaves, and wither at his feet.
How could he tell of fleeting hopes and fears,
Of myriad passing loves, and woes, and wars !
Emmets and men, teeming and vanishing,
In halls of stone, or tunnell'd, chamber'd hills,
Or wattled huts, as here ! men's thrilling lives
Gleam, firefly-like, a moment wonderful ;
Frail, nor so blithe as yon fair living lights,
That are and are not in the fragrant shade.

And since she died,[12] rapture of my young
    years,
Love, and abiding pole-star of my life!
A marble cross, that gleams amid the gloom
Shines ever in dim vistas of my soul;
And I desire to lay my toil-worn limbs
Under still leaves of some primæval grove,
As she, my well-beloved, resteth hers.
She sail'd from England, to divide my care,
With brave Mackenzie's and another's wife:
Alas! Mackenzie and his friend had fallen
In the stern path of duty when they came!
And these two white-faced women wept alone
Over two very silent forest graves.
Alas! how soon I wept beside another;
For very soon my Mary went to rest.
(Her venerable father, Moffat, only
Is known among the tribes of Africa
As my own Mary's father, as Ra-Mary.)
The fever seized her, and she pass'd away:
She pass'd at sunset on a Sabbath eve,
And left my feet to wander in the shade.

Upon a gentle, green acclivity,
Under a venerable Mowana tree,
Garlanded with odorous flowers,
Tranquil in the sunny hours,
          She sleeps in glory !

Orchards of mango basking in the south ;
Northward fair palm, and many a noble growth
Of oriental forest tree,
Where silvern Liambayee
          Wanders in glory ;

On his fair bosom many a sunny isle,
Calm as herself within the heavenly smile :
Upon the marble of her grave
Mowana shadows gently wave,
          Waver in glory.

Pearly light clouds about his purple form,
High in the azure, deep, and wide, and warm,
Mount Morambala soareth high,
Serene in mountain majesty,
          Dreaming in glory :

Gleam forth, O marble, from the wilding gloom !
Shine, O white cross, upon the martyr's tomb !
Faithful toil, long-suffering care,
Radiate over dark and fair,
            Burst into glory !

CANTO IV.

 CANNOT loathe nor scorn the colour'd
            man ;
        Nor deem him far below my Master's
            love.
I know about the sutures of his skull ;
But I have proved him verily my brother.
And I have heard of Toussaint L'Ouverture !
(Perchance I am not so fastidious
As those who have great genius for words ;
Yet we dumb doers crave some standing room,
O ye, so deft and dazzling with the tongue !)

Well I remember, after all my toil,
When within grasp of a momentous prize,
Earth seem'd to glide from under ; all was failing,
Even as now ! my very faithful friends—
Who had plunged in drowning floods to rescue me ;
Who had interposed their bodies to avert
The deadly javelin aim'd against my life ;
Who, pressing princely favours on my need,
With more than counsel, with material aid,
Further'd my humanizing pilgrimage ; [13]
When Christian Levites would have pass'd me by,
Jingled their gold, and sneer'd " Utopia ! "—
My welltried Makololo, *they* desert me !
Shrinking at last from more long sacrifice,
Bitter and boundless, it may be unavailing—
I shall not reach those Lusian settlements
Upon the long'd-for coast ! all urge return.
.   .   .   .   Return I will not !
" Return *ye* then, my people !   I will go
Alone, if so indeed it needs must be ! "
With heavy tread, with heavier heart, I enter,
Weary and fever-stricken, my small tent

Under a tamarind; and I lean my head
Upon my hand to offer up a prayer.
Silence is all around me in the noon—
Yet only for a little—then I hear
Footsteps approaching; timidly one peers,
And sees me by the tent-pole; first the one,
Then more, have push'd the canvas fold aside;
Falling upon me like repentant children,
Sobbing, with tears they pray to be forgiven :
" We never meant it !   We will never leave thee !
" Our own kind Father ! be of better cheer !
" Where'er thou leadest, we will follow thee ! "

And that poor African, who when I sail'd
For England supplicated to be taken !
It was with bleeding heart I said him nay.
I told him he would perish of the cold
In my bleak country, but he sobb'd with tears :
" O let me come, and perish at your feet ! "
Sebweku had a stronger claim than he.
Alas ! Sebweku !
The sea was rolling mountains high, when all

Embark'd at Kilimane in a boat.
Ascending gliding turbid mountain-slopes,
Their toppling hissing foamy summits broke
Drenching upon us, and submerged our bark :
Giddily slid we deep into the trough,
Whose seething waterwalls hid all the masts
Of that great vessel which awaited us :
We struck the massy bottom with a shock,
That made our stout planks quiver; slanting up
Another beetling journeying watercliff,
Second of three great billows lightning-crown'd.
Poor Sebweku, so valiant on land,
So wise and skill'd in dealing with the many
Tribes of his continent, strove strenuously
To be as brave in my fierce water world,
Ghostly, unknown, terrific unto him :
Yet as that awful play of leaping foam
Struck us, and nearly swept us all from life,
He clutch'd my knees, crying with face of fear,
Faintly illumed by a poor phantom smile,
Like a wet timid gleam among wan clouds,
" Is this the way you go ? is this the way ? "

But when we had made a perilous ascent
Into the British war-brig anchor'd near,
His fresh fantastic marvelling child-soul,
So little tutor'd, ponder'd evermore
On all he saw within the war vessel ;
Cannon, great coils of cable, ponderous chain,
Hammocks, and kitchen of the floating town,
Her sailors, and well-order'd soldiery ;
On the interminable water world,
Strewn with dark swimming snakes, and plants ;
   where roll
Dolphins and whales ; where azure fishes fly,
And birds gleam in a momentary ray
Out of dull storm that raves among the shrouds.
Reeling to starboard and to larboard, he,
By swaying lamplight, in the midnight hour,
Lies wakeful, hearing labouring timbers groan,
Or shouted orders, piercing all the roar ;
And clear struck bells, dividing hour from hour.
He, creeping up lone glimmering hatchway stairs,
Beholds a gleam from that mysterious shrine
Where, under lighted crystal, a slim needle

F

Trembles for ever toward the hidden pole;
Notes a bronzed mariner's strong vigilance
Revolving with both arms the straining wheel,
Beyond wet decks, wash'd over by fierce seas;
Beholds tall masts, more tall than forest kings,
Robed in broad shadowy windy sails and booms,
Circling among wan stars in rifts of cloud.

All made him welcome, and they liked him well;
But the new wonderworld inflamed his brain;
Kept his mind whirling ever night and day;
Until, when we approach'd Mauritius,
A steamer steam'd from forth the harbour
      mouth—
Wonder of wonders to poor Sebweku !
Fiery smoke outbursting from her funnel,
She churns the water with a rushing wheel;
Slanting and swiftly swims upon the wave :
He cries : " It is some fiend of the wild sea ! "
Alas ! my friend. .   .   .   .
    .   .   .   .   When we are calmly moor'd,
In a mad frenzy plunges—and is drown'd !

And yet my negroes at a later day[14]
Proved boldest, skilfullest of mariners.
Perilously braving mountainous ocean-waves,
And howling winds, our tight but tiny craft,
Lady Nyassa, from Mozambique flew,
Resolved to harbour in far Asia.
Mine own hands ruled the helm, my sleepless eyes
Watching the needle : often would we clutch
Fast, lest some phantom billow whirl us forth ;
Hurrying, swirling, billows playing with us,
Whose foam-fangs gleam'd in night's chaotic war !
But my blithe monkey-nimble negro boys,
While our spars heaving dipp'd in hissing sea,
Climb'd undismay'd, and clinging, deftly reeved
A rope, at my bawl'd orders, through a block ;
With ebony heads and frames immersed in brine,
Held their brave breaths ; then with the rope be-
    tween
White, shining teeth, return'd triumphantly.
When by a miracle we made the port ;
Nor founder'd, leaving ne'er a living soul
To tell the tale ; among tall mast-forests

In that great hazy harbour of Bombay,
None could discover, though they sought for long,
Where our wee " Lady" had bestow'd herself!

How glorious and amiable some scenes
Of gorgeous loveliness, and human joy,
That pass before mine inner eyes to-night!
For there is unsophisticated joy,
Yea, hardy virtue in rude nature's child;
And there are sins, with poignant miseries,
Our subtler, jaded brains impart to him.
Witness, the desolation and despair[15]
Of guileless peoples, beautiful and kind,
Basking in smiles of bounteous mother Earth,
Wrought by pale Spaniards; whom they held
            divine,
Descended from the crystal firmament,
In silks and flashing armour, on white wings
Of golden galleons; offering on their knees
Flowers and fruits and spices of their isle!
And you, ye murderers of Patteson!
Not poor blind islanders, but English fiends!

Beware, O ye who follow after me,
Of how ye deal with this, mine Africa!

Methinks I hear some solemn state palaver,
Held in the grand unwall'd assembling-place,
Thatch'd with bamboos and branches, when blue
     morn
Glows golden, while cool shadows at the doors
Of a leaf-bower'd village minish fast.
Morn lies a lake of light amid the bloom
And billowy wealth of forest foliage;
Young Sun, ascending, shines on thatch like snow,
Revealing veins of herbs, and draining them;
Glancing among high senatorial boughs
Of feathery tamarind, or mahogany;
While dews of slumber rustle rainbow rain
In sylvan, solitary silences
Of Nature's own cathedral sanctuary.
A spear is in the dusky orator's hand,
And spears are planted black athwart the day;
Dark bearded elders hearken solemnly,
Resting on logs, all polish'd from long use.

Perennial founts of eloquent, warm words
Are these untutor'd children of the sun !

Now reigns the blazing furnace of full noon :
And save for little rills that want no sleep,
Silence, before the intolerable glory,
Falls on a cowering world of beast and man.
Bird-song has waned, and even the stridulent
Cicala sleeps ; a rare bee drowsily
Explores a twilit labyrinth of flowers ;
Delicate blossoms dallying in warm airs,
Bowing and yielding to the velvet lover ;
While heaven-blue elves with pulsing fans alight
Over a ruin of red leaves, or sail
From light to shadow, like a jubilant
Song, failing in a tenderer low minor.
Gorgeous insects of metallic gleam
Waver, and glance, and glimmer on the fronds.
Low, murmurous sound pervades all emerald aisles,
As   though   the   floral   earth   and   leaves   were
          breathing.
Life teems ! a myriad hidden mandibles,

Amid lush herbage, under moss and loam,
Clear away life superfluous, and death.
Gorgeous fungi here and there reveal,
Where sun can pierce, traversing shadows thrown
Athwart them from some silken spider's line,
To and fro glancing when a zephyr breathes ;
Bending long grasses wheresoe'er it hangs.
And hark ! the honey-bird invites to steal
Delicious honey-combs from hollow boles.

Hearken again !
A sound, how plaintive and melodious,
Swells in the green gloom ! it is like one note
From a sweet vibrant lyre—a hidden bird !

Women have gone, with infants slung behind
    them,
Toward a spring, light pitchers gracefully
Poised on their heads by steadying of dark arms
Curl'd over ; or they bruise with iron hoes
The hopeful soil ; plant yams and manioc ;
Pound in wood mortars these, or maize and millet ;

Hem with some thorn, or fish-bone for a needle,
And fibres of a leaf; weave grassy cloths
In looms, or spin with immemorial spindle.
Some men have gone with quiver, targe, and spear,
To hunt the beast for food; some loll at ease,
Like their own gourds, luxuriously idle;
Listless and vacant dumb black animals,
Who spurn the accursèd yoke of thought and toil—
They never roll the stone of Sisyphus!
No fool's ambition ever goads their lives
To rouse a restless rumour, while they roll
Into fate's mortal darkness, and to leave
A hollow murmur for a little time
In some poor space of insignificant earth!

Now Sun steals westward; and his fading light
Glows golden, while cool shadows at the doors
Of leaf-embower'd villages are long.
Burning he falls into the forest sea,
Inflames leaf-billows with purpureal fire;
Drawing down souls to caves of the under-world;
Whence in twelve hours he royal will arise

From holy nenuphars upon the river !
Fragrance and song, released from royalty
Of his fierce presence, timid lift their heads ;
Grey parrots crying flutter home to roost.
Hunters return, with many a gay halloo,
And whoop light-hearted, bearing various game,
About whose way hilarious women throng,
Calling them by pet names, and fondling them,
Prattling, intent to hear of all the sport.
Boys in gourd bowls bring frothy plantain wine
From cool leaf-cellars in low boughs of trees,
Presenting it with clapping of their hands :
Anon there smokes a savoury repast,
Viands of venison, nuts, and season'd yams.

Dancing and singing under tender stars,
In serene purple air ! a rising moon
Charming all harshness from the fuming flame
Of resinous torch, and lowlier village fires,
Mild as evanishing fireflies in the shade !
A night of love for lovely youths and girls,
Of revelry, and wine and flute playing,

Psaltery, reed, marimba, or cithern ;
Rude sires of more harmonious instruments,
String'd with a root, a snake-skin strain'd
    athwart—
One sang me a small song about the dance.

    The dance ! the dance !
    Maidens advance
    Your undulating charm !
    A line deploys
    Of gentle boys,
    Waving the light arm,
    Bronze alive and warm ;
    Reedflute and drum
    Sound as they come,
    Under your eyelight warm !

    Many a boy,
    A dancing joy,
    Many a mellow maid,
    With fireflies in the shade,
    Mingle and glide,
    Appear and hide,

Here in a fairy glade :
Ebb and flow
To a music low,
Viol, and flute and lyre,
As melody mounts higher :
With a merry will,
They touch and thrill,
Beautiful limbs of fire !

Red berries, shells,
Over bosom-dells,
And girdles of light grass,
May never hide
The youthful pride
Of beauty, ere it pass :
Yet, ah ! sweet boy and lass,
Refrain, retire !
Love is a fire !
Night will pass !

I came to pleasant places on my way !
Lawns of deep verdure by a silvern water ;
Wind-waved savannahs flush'd with floral bloom,

Clouded with saffron or cerulean flowers,
And little silken blossoms of pure snow,
Dying in dews of every dying eve,
Living in all revivals of the morn.
Here women singing reap the golden grain,
Or bind in sheaves; here flourish cotton-fleece,
Rice, tendrill'd peas, and pulse, and sugar-cane ;
While mottled kine, knee-deep in flowering
        grasses,
At milking time low to their prison'd heifers,
And merry kidlings frisk at bower'd doors.
The men under some fig's rich canopy
Sit weaving limber baskets, or a weir,
And fishing-creel.
                Slight palisades preserve
Dark jasper-jewell'd women, as they fill
Their pitchers in the river, from the foul
Scaled alligators that abound below,
Watchfully lurking underneath wan water ;
Dim treacherous shadows, motionless like stone,
Monsters who linger from primæval time,
Ere man appear'd to rule—

Nay, some still pay them tribute of a prayer ;
Offer their very little ones to soothe
And sate bestial malign divinities !
These have their priest, temple, and sacrifice,
Or priestess, with observances impure :
So have green serpents, tongued with flickering fire,
Whose stealthy glide flames out in torturing
    hells. . .
. . Are these dark aberrations of the soul
Terrible legacies bequeathed to men
By some forefather of Egyptian race,
Who bore the ritual of his ancient realm
To these far wilds of Ethiopia ?—
Bringing his cast of feature, and the modes
Of intricate hairbraids involved with bark ;
Manners of tilling earth and harvesting,
Spindles, and ways of weaving warp with weft. —
Or was it some primæval ancestor,
Common to all, whom so the Lord made wise,
And whom in turn the Enemy beguiled ?
But still, upon broad shoulders of strong men,
A sacred ark is borne at the full moon

Among dark faces of adoring crowds,
Moonsilver'd, lit from lamps of gourd or melon,
Amid glad music and loud clapping hands ;
Even as in Saïs, at the Feast of Lamps,
Far away in dim hollows of the past !

Among rare visions of celestial glory,
And all responsive splendours upon Earth,
In such a scene as these, in such a river,
Behold ! a maiden in her earliest prime
Bound to a stake, bare-limb'd upon a bank,
The ripple washing over her slim ankles,
And lovely swaying lilies kissing them.
She horror-frozen waits the horrid doom . .
. . A hideous head protrudes from forth the shoal :
There is a whirl of monstrous dragon-tail . .
. . Andromeda's red blood afflicts the river ;
Whom no fair wingèd Perseus may save !

I travell'd over many lakes and rivers,
In floating trees men hollow'd with an adze
For a canoe, my rowers with wild song

Paddling or poling, in accordant time
Of oar and voice, chanting some ancient stave
Of river-song in tones Gregorian,
Solemn and strange, ancient as Pharaoh !

How wonderful it was to float along the river !
Dreamily hearing water plash and gurgle
From my canoe's advancing sides and oars,
Washing among green rushes of the shore !
Wherein wing'd warblers, plumed in spousal hues
Of green, gold, scarlet, sable, white and azure,
Flash'd, thrill'd, and warbled; here in the Summer-
        land,
Now in the latest of two fairy summers,
When there is snow in England—ah ! and bells ;
With lovelier light and warmth of home and
        heart !
Hark ! how they sing to soft mates in nests woven
Of green flags, nimble bills have sown with webs ;
While, sunning them, they preen their little wings,
Showering drops that trickle down the stems !
Earlier rains have fallen ; a fresh air

Fans clear and lucid now in morning hours ;
Vivid green pennons of tall rushes wave
Athwart blue light, with dense papyrus reed,
Wherein soft brown gazelles rustle and play
'Neath hollyhock, brown bulrush, and flagflowers.
A mighty river horse
Protrudes a shining snout ; trumpets aloud,
Blowing out spurts of water like a whale.
" *Pula, pula,*" calls the " Son-in-law of God ; " [16]
While ever and anon an ebony bird
Rouses from his dim dreaming on the sand,
And screaming harshly, wakes a long wild cry
From some fish-eagle, widening vast brown wings.
In shoals grave marabouts, with red flamingoes,
Wade ; and behold ! yon bird on floating lotus
Leaves walks among the holy white lilies,
Dipping a glossy fold below the ripple.
A snowy ibis, a slim demoiselle,
A tall grey heron, an egret of white plume ;
These, and the like, stand fairy sentinels,
With wavering bright image down below,
Silent before a twilit emerald

Of river margin, radiant in bloom.
Yellow milola, blue convolvulus,
Whose vases seem to overflow with heaven,
These all are haunts of lustrous dragon-fly ;
Gorgeous velvet moth, sipping the sweet ;
Of dappled bees, gold-dusted ; butterflies,
Wing'd like the train of Juno's heavenly bird.

Onward we glide, and twine meandering
On a moss-colour'd water, till the gale
Relieves my merry rowers ; we expand
A little sail, filling with soft sweet air,
Like some soft bird's white bosom heaved with
        song,
White as a foam of waterfalls ; we glide
Merrily among wave-enchanted flowers,
Glossily heaving while we gently pass ;
Or splendid twinkling trees, immersed in light,
From shadowy bosoms offering fruits of Eden ;
Breathing a perfume as of Paradise
From their soft islands ; islands of the blest,
Bower'd to the marge, re-echo'd in the water ;

With many a fleecy cloudlet sailing slow.
Small richly armour'd quaint iguanas bask
On every sunniest bough; while startled eyes
Of glorious lithe beasts flash for a moment
Out of the solemn sylvan opaline
Of hoary forest boles, and swiftly vanish:
Little agamas nod their orange heads;
A lovely praying mantis, green as leaves,
Rests on green leaves; and green cameleons.

We wind along; the waters rise from rain;
Blue hazy hills arise, saluting us.
Often, when we have doubled some fair cape,
With thud and plash fall fragments of rich loam;
And as we round low river promontories,
Crocodiles basking upon yellow sand,
With dull green eyes, and huge obscene fang'd
      jaws,
Wake startled; gliding plunge into the flood;
Where many a delicate-tinted pelican
Stores silver fishes in his hanging pouch.

Wandering devious, many-mooded rivers
Mazily saunter, with a floating flower,
Or leaf, or bubble on their bosom borne;
With labyrinthine silver in the blue;
Indolent dimpling playful light and shadow;
Now washing swiftly round about the roots
Of guava, mango, fountainous cocoa-palm,
Or palm that, veil'd in climbing green llianas,
High over all the verdure lifts a spire.
Among blithe rapids my dark boatmen wade,
Merrily pushing; while at waterfalls,
Pendent in green woods among roseate rocks,
Pendent, like plumes of birds of paradise,
They carry our frail bark upon their shoulders.

Sunset arrives : a stilly-flowing flood
Glows, like blent molten metals brilliant,
Dark and light green, crimson, purple and gold,
Repeating heaven; as though yon gleaming beetles,
Swaying among the verdure, were afloat,
One solid army of them, mail'd in glory.

I enter equatorial lakes, unknown,
To any European eyes before :
Ngami, Bemba, Moero, Nyassa ;
Slumbering in grand enfolding arms
Of old volcanic mountain, tempest-crown'd !
Profound and lonely children of the waters,
Whom gorgeous-vestured giant forms o'erfrown,
Bastion, tower, inviolate precipice,
Burying them from all-beholding Sun
In sullen shadow, many hours a year.
Ngami ! earliest lake mine eyes beheld ;
On whose fair shores of old exultantly
I stood, with my dear little ones and *her !*
This inland sea, this noble Tanganika,
Where Burton came with Speke, whom England
        mourns,
Hath all his guardian mountains foliaged
From wave to heaven ; magnificently robed
In rich luxuriant foliage of Mvulé,
And other alien blossoming tall trees,
Bauhinia, tamarind, teak, and sycomore,
Enfolding purple torrent-cloven ravines.

While otherwhere long sheeny rapier blades
Of green matete cane adorn the marge,
With mangroves, whose bare roots affect the fen.
One who rows softly, rounding promontories,
When these high hills are overarch'd with azure,
Dipping his paddle in a light blue water,
Beholds embower'd in sweet shingly coves
Palm-nestled, hive-like huts and villages,
Whose dwellers ply their busy crafts on shore,
While fishing gear and boats adorn the strand . . .
. . And what if this great water gender Nile ? [17]
For I have seen a Northward drift of boughs,
With other floating waifs ; while Arabs tell
How from far Northern limits of the lake
A river floweth North—perchance to where
Baker, with his heroic consort, came ? . .
. . Where issueth else the mighty water forth ?

[18] MOSI-OA-TUNYA.

Smooth river water holdeth softly furl'd
Thee, hoarded wonder of the wondrous world !

Ere thy tempestuous cataracts are hurl'd,
    Mosi-oa-tunya !

Twenty miles away thy sound
Travels from the gulf profound
Of thine earth-convulsing bound,
    Mosi-oa-tunya !

Five great cloudy columns rise,
To uphold the rolling skies :
Morning clothes with rainbow dyes
    •Mosi-oa-tunya !

Awful phantoms in the moon
Rise to thy tremendous tune :
·When the fiery evening falls,
Hell sulphureous appalls,
While thy blazing thunder calls,
    Mosi-oa-tunya !

The huge Mowana, and the Mohonono,
Like silvery cedar-trees on Lebanon,
Wave, with light palms, upon the pleasant isles

And shores, ere Leeambayee vanishes,
As though annihilate in his proud career:
Motsouri-cypress, yielding scarlet fruit;
All noblest equatorial trees adorn
His mile-wide water, clear as a clear day,
Gliding like lightning into the abyss.

Clear a moment, ere thou blanch
Into a mile-wide avalanche,
Snowfall lapsing twice the height
Of Niagara in his might!
Born of thy resounding day,
Myriad meteors o'er thee play:
There is an evergreen dark grove,
Guarded by thine own awful love:
Her inner melancholy no sun may move,
Mosi-oa-tunya!

Tall ghostly forms of sounding cloud
Clothe her in a rainbow shroud;
No bird of hers carols aloud,
Mosi-oa-tunya!

Down the rock's tremendous face,
Foam-rills, tremulous like lace,
Flow from roots that grasp the place,
To where thy vaporous cauldrons hiss;
But ere they may attain to this,
Smoke roaring, whirl'd from the abyss,
Licks them off precipitous stone,
High into a cloudy zone,
            Mosi-oa-tunya !

Water and wind jamm'd in a chasm profound,
Tortured, pent-up, and madden'd, with strong
      sound
War in world-ruining chaos, fierce rebounding ;
A wild tumultuous rumour, earth and heaven con-
      founding.

After, the river rushes, a long green
Serpent, convolved about dark promontories
Of sternest basalt, in the unfathomable
Chasm to and fro, a swift fork'd lightning-flash ;
B ut all the promontories are crown'd with trees,

Gorgeous blooming herbage and tall flowers.

On a green island, hanging o'er the flood,
Even where it falleth, lovely flowers are wooed,
And with eternal youth imbued,
By a lapse of gentle rain
From the cataract's hurricane :
Love celestial in showers
Falls from devastating powers !
Under the foam-bow and the cloud,
Here where thunders peal aloud,
Human souls with trembling bow'd,
      Mosi-oa-tunya !

Cruel lords of all the isles,
Though a heavenly rainbow smiles,
Only feel bewildering annihilating terror ;
Offer human lives to thee in blind, bewilder'd error.
Love abideth still, sublime
O'er the roar and whirl of Time,
Foam-bow of a sunnier clime,
      Mosi-oa-tunya !

But I behold there, on high poles exposed,
White skulls of strangers, whom the savage
    hordes
Of river-pirates most inhumanly
Slew: these barbarians the Makololo,
Sebituane, routed and destroy'd ;
Planting his own Bechuana speech abroad
Among the nations; opening thereby .
A way wherein our Sacred Oracles
May march triumphant, blessing all the land ;
Since Moffat arduously render'd them
Into a heretofore unletter'd tongue.

By moonlight, or by starlight, when we pause
Upon the river's bosom, ah ! how fair !
Shadowy fruits and flowers in elf-light hanging ;
Plaintive low voices floating tenderly.
One waking here, in slumber borne from far,
Would deem he had died in sleep, and was in
    heaven.

Alas! all fair dreams fade, and this would fade !

Joy only masketh the wan face of woe.
For not alone here fever's mortal breath
Chills all exultant ardours of the brave ;
Slackens bent bows of young impetuous lives,
Baffling the swift-wing'd arrows of their aim ;
Veils youthful eyes in languorous impotence,
So that they love no more fair life than death.
But there is worse than treacherous-soul'd
      Miasma,
Lurking for prey, close-mask'd in orient glory,
Enveloping a man with subtle folds
Of dull impalpable mortality.
Sin is a deadlier malady than all !
These flowers are only strewn upon a corpse.
Man has made Earth a hissing and a scorn
Among the constellated worlds of light !
And here the plague-spot is the loathliest.

I have come to pleasant places on my way :
Angels beholding might be lured from heaven !
And in the course of my long wandering
I have return'd once more to visit them.

Alas ! how changed !

. . Bowery villages roll volumed clouds

Of fiery smoke, staining the limpid light;

Rich harvests, charr'd, or trampled, or ungarner'd

Idly luxuriant, meet the mournful eye.

While, even beside a fair golden array

Of bounteous corn, a few starved boys and women,

Gaunt as yon skeletons around them strewn,

Crawl; listless, hopeless famine in their eyes;

All that were dear, slain, tortured, or expell'd

By arm'd assaults of the fierce slave-driver.

And ah ! these skeletons ! the tales they tell !

Beside fair river-banks, beside wreck'd huts,

Under green trees, under red rocks, in caves,

Ghastly anatomies, in attitudes

Of mortal anguish, writhed, and curl'd, and

        twisted,

Mutually clasp'd in transports of despair !

In one closed cabin, when mine eyes conform

To its faint twilight, on a rude raised bed

Appear two skeletons in mouldering weeds;

The head of one fallen from its wooden pillow ;
And piteous between them a small form
Of a starved child, nestled by sire and mother.
The dead, and living wounded, and the babes,
Are flung by those contemptuous conquerors
To feed loathsome hyenas, that assemble
Through lurid smoke of sunset, gaunt and grey ;
With obscene screaming vultures, heavily
Wheeling, or swooping; rending the live prey.
One infant darling, weeping, wilder'd, still
Solicits the cold breast of a dead mother !

I have seen Lualaba's mighty rolling water
Red with the blood of a blithe innocent people,
Who, unforeboding slant-eyed treachery,
Chaffer'd, and bought and sold, as was their wont,
In a populous fair by the worn river-marge.
And there was melody of mandolin,
And dulcet flute ; with dancing, and warm love
Of gay young lovers, under broad brown eaves,
Sheltering from a hot ascending day :
Where clear young laughter blent deliciously

With falling notes of bowery turtle-doves,
Mantled in hues of tender summer cloud.
Hearken !—a rush ! a trample of arm'd men !
A sudden deafening crash of musketry !
Hundreds of blithe love-dreaming youths and
      maidens,
Bathed in their own life-blood, and one another's,
Fall, with one last death-quivering embrace :
While women in rude violating arms
Of strangers struggle ; and the flower of men
Strain their necks impotent in yokes of iron,
Grappled around them by their insolent foes.
Hundreds in panic blind—man, woman, child—
Plunge among waters of deep Lualaba ;
Whose drowning bodies the swift current hurries ;
These, maim'd swollen corpses, drifting far away,
Hideously-croaking famish'd alligators
Fight for portentous ; lashing furious trains,
Pulling asunder human trunks and limbs !

But follow ye the stolen journeying slave !
Behold her toiling shackled, starved, and goaded

Upon her weary way through wild and wood,
Under the sunblaze ; till her bleeding feet
Refuse their office ; till she faints and falls !
Whom the tormentors, with a curse and jeer,
Torture to sense of cruel life once more :
Two burdens doth she carry ; one, her babe :
She cannot bear them both ; they snatch the babe
From her, for all the wailing and wrung hands ;
Tossing it crush'd upon a mossy stone.
They goad her on ; full blinding tears have
  darken'd
All the parch'd earth; she cannot stumble far—
Now shouts arise to kill her—it is done !
Christ saith to Satan : " Hold ! the child shall
 . sleep !"

CANTO V.

OLEMNLY purple night reigns over
me,
With all the solemn glory of her stars.
Sublime star-worlds, who never have
disdain'd
To be my friends, consolers, counsellors,
Guiding faint footfalls of a mortal man !
How often, when the moon among your lights
Glided, with her wan face beholding day ;
A slim canoe, carven from tender pearl,
Confused to many crescents as I gaze ;
Noting the very punctual moment, I
Besought my faithful sextant to reveal
What interval of cavernous clear gloom
Lay now between her orb and one of you !
I found how high above your brilliant
Image in my small pool of mercury

Ye rose in heaven on my meridian.
So, in the least conjectured realm of all
These pilgrim feet have found, my whereabout
On this our Earth discovering I record.
But the barbarians, when they saw me place
And note the readings of mine instrument,
Deemed me magician; some beneath their breath,
Viewing my quadrant's ivory curvature,
Whisper'd: " The Son of God hath come to us ;
And lo! the moon was underneath his arm !
He holdeth strange communion with stars."

Yours are fair faces of familiar friends
To the lone traveller in a lonely land,
Ye constellations, slowly journeying west !
And some of you, my best beloved at home
May not behold; but some of you, with me,
Their eyes and mine may gaze upon together.
Glorious worlds, unknown to mortal men,
My spirit yearns to you from hollow orbs !
Soon shall I slake my longing all divine
Even in you, with higher powers than these

H

Of this poor worn-out body !

                Now my soul

Seeks those immortals, who have passed away

From earth to yonder infinite star-worlds :

World within world, sun, planet, comet, moon,

All in their order and their own degree,

One crimson, and one golden, and one green,

Harmonious hearing a low voice of Love !

Star of the Nile ! resplendent Sirius !

Whom here men name " Drawer of all the

    Night ! "

Planet of Love ! Ntanda,[19] fair firstborn

Of evening, tremulous dew in a sweet rose !

(She is so large, and clear, she sheds a shadow :)

Aldebaran, Orion, Fomalhaut,

Altair, Canopus, and the Southern Cross !

    Now fades yon pyramid of nebulous light

Zodiacal, that, paling as it soars,

Tinges mild splendour of the Milky Way

A delicate orange ; but Magellan's clouds

Revolve around our starless Southern Pole.

And all is silence—only a night air
Rustles a palm, dreaming among the stars,
From whose dim languorous long fronds they
      rise,
Slow disentangling their celestial gleam.
No human sound disturbs the solitude.
Only a cry of some far florican ;
A chirping cricket in the herb afar,
Or doleful forest-muffled living thing.
Also I hear a distant ghostly voice
Of plangent surf, alternately resounding
And ceasing, on wild Tanganyika's shore.
But some low thunder booms at intervals.
Some say it is a surge, wandering in caves
Unfathomable of a mighty mountain range,
Far off to westward, nearer Liembâ.
And some affirm a river under earth
Rushes in yonder mountains of Kabongo,
Breathing a strange low thunder on the
      wind . . .
England ! my children ! shall I see you once
Again before I perish ?—nay the end

Is very near : here I shall die alone :
I am weary, worn, deserted, destitute !

It may be that my work is nearly done.
And though some say Christ cannot conquer here,
A noble army of dark men to-day,
Following His banner, proudly spurn the lie.
The native chief Sechele,[20] whom I taught,
Now teaches all his subject countrymen ;
And Africaner, the black conqueror,
Whose very name was terror to the world
Of his resistless ruining career,
Moffat alone, no weapon in his hand,
Subdued with silent spiritual power.
The haughty devastating spirit bow'd,
Like Saul of old, a willing thrall to Christ ;
So that all marvell'd to behold the man,
Saying, " Can this indeed be Africaner ? "
I have unveil'd before the feeble eyes,
Inured to twilight of a prison cell,
Little by little, His fair radiance,
Reflecting Him, though faintly, in my life.

Also I made myself as one of them,
Seeking the bent and habit of their souls,
That I might govern, order, set to use.

And I would have wise lovers of mankind,
Dwelling through all the land in colonies ;
Gendering new necessities of life,
Desires entwined with all the nobler growth
Of reason, mutual reverence, and love ;
Arousing men with sturdier enterprise
To stir the virtues of a virgin soil ;
Fostering civil arts of mutual peace,
That ask for interchange of services.
So shall they cherish honourable trade
In all the wealth of Ethiopia ;
Ebony, amber, gold, and ivory ;
A care to barter these for what is wrought
By fiery familiars of the brain
Yonder in Europe, in our world sublime
Of godlike labour, triumph, and despair ;
In realms more wonderful than Africa !
For in our Europe and America,

Sun, ocean, earth, are vassals unto man ;
For whom he moulds huge organs all inform'd
With a blind emanation from the soul—
Wheel within wheel of giant enginery,
Thunderously storming, wailing, murmuring,
Cow'd slaves of his creative human will ;
Eager to mangle the slight taskmaster,
If God plunge him among their whirling limbs. . .

But with a gauntlet of stern iron crush out,
England ! the foul snake coil'd voluminous
About this desolate land, feeding on blood !
Forbid, stamp out, the accursed trade in men :
Nor dare neglect the mission of the strong,
To bind the oppressor, and to help the poor !

Then shall these glorious immemorial rivers,
And inland seas, mine eyes have first beholden,
The Lord's highways of holiness and peace,
Alive with white-wing'd ministers of heaven,
Waft sunnier glory to the jubilant shores
Of Ethiopia, and the Maurian's land

Lift up her dark deliver'd hands to God !
I may not see it ! Like Israel's leader, I
Am but a pioneer to bring the people
Out of their bondage : as on Pisgah's height,
I may behold the promised land from far. . .
I have flung wide the portals of the night :
Children of hope and morning, enter ye ! "

CANTO VI.

OW daylight rules: but Livingstone
still sleeps
Within the clay-built shadowy cham-
ber walls.
Fragments of torn soil'd paper, strewn around,
Show notes of travel jotted on the way
With his own red blood, used in place of ink.
A notebook, and a Bible, lie beside ;
With sextant, and chronometer, and hides ;
Ivory, tusks, a rifle, a javelin.

Hark ! the tranquillity of burning noon
A distant shot disturbs !—and now another !
Men rouse them—what is it ? another shot !
It must be some approaching caravan.
Shall they awake the Master ?   Nay, he hears :
He is awake, and, listening, wonders too ;
Hoping, and fearing ; communing with God.
He sends his trusted servant to discover
Who is the leader of the caravan.
He has heard rumours of a white man near.
Who ? can he be commissioned to relieve ?
" 'Tis only some pale trader after all ! "
The messenger in breathless haste returns :
He has seen the leader of the coming band :
" It is a white man ! and he seeks for thee,
My Master ! he hath large supplies with him ! "
But Livingstone can scarce believe for joy.
And yet what grateful accents from afar
Come faintly wafted on this Afric air ?
A hearty ringing Anglo-Saxon cheer !
Renew'd by multitudinous followers,
Advancing down the forested hill-sides

Of Ukaranga ! swiftly they arrive :
Eager Ujiji pours excitedly
To give the strangers greeting—a black crowd,
Among dim huts and trees, with bearded grave,.
Flowing-robed, turban'd Arabs, in the rear
Of England's great explorer, waiting now
To welcome his unknown deliverer.
How ? 'tis the banner of America !
America saves England—mighty Child
Of mighty Mother, it is nobly done !
Join your two strong right hands for evermore,.
And swear that none shall sever them anew !
Then tremble, crown'd oppressors of mankind !
England, America, on your free soil
The slave may kneel ; but only kneel to God !
Thou, gallant Stanley, scorning toil, alert,
Stern battling with thy formidable foes,
Hast won the brilliant prize ; and Europe turns
Her enviously grateful eyes on thee !

The outer world supposed the traveller dead.
But Murchison, and some true friends beside,

In England, as beyond the sundering sea,
Firm in sagacious confidence, divined
His living need, and sent strong hearts to help.
Young, namesake of a faithful friend at home,[21]
Finds all the falsehood of a traitor's tale :
But Stanley finds the murder'd man alive !
His ardent spirit bounds with generous joy,
Proudly exultant; for himself hath found
The man whom Europe and America
Delight to honour, and desire to save.

Who should this be with venerable mien,
And ashen hair, and worn wan countenance,
Travel-marr'd, in dun raiment, with bowed form,
Wearing a mariner's goldbanded cap ;
Of aspect firm, beneficent, and calm ;
He who advances with a kindly smile
Before the Arabs ?—'tis a stranger's face—
Yet Stanley knows it must be Livingstone !
Longing to clasp him in a friend's embrace,
And yet restraining transports honourable,
He only bares the deeply reverent head,

With questioning accent naming the great name.
Livingstone warmly grasps the proffer'd hand.
And after salutation courteous
To some around, these recent yet fast friends
Turn toward the claybuilt tembé; whose broad eaves
This afternoon shall shelter two glad men,
In place of one alone and desolate.
The traveller, slowly dying yesterday,
Now shares with relish in a plenteous meal,
Reiterating : " You have brought me life ! "

Letters from loved ones, how long silent ! soon
The pilgrim reads ; and while soft evening wears,
They sit communing of how many things !
They speak of friends ; of some whom fame well
          knows ;
And one whom Livingstone may chance to name
Yet lives—another—he has pass'd away !
Then the explorer tells a wondrous tale
Of his exploits, adventures, and desires.
But on himself, emerged but yesterday
From forests of the dark barbarian,

His comrade pours a flood of radiance
From royal Europe trembling to her base,
And deluged in the lifeblood of her sons—
France, the Colossus, shatter'd at Sedan ;
Her emperor, with all her chivalry,
Slain, or enthrall'd ; while Germany the proud
Draws stern inveterate coils of battle close
About the fairest city in the world !
Moltke and Bismarck are dismembering France ;
William assumes old Barbarossa's crown
In that great mirror'd chamber of the halls,
Which Louis, Gaul's grand monarch, piled in
    pride
To all the glories of his conquering race !

The wanderer listens, marvelling, to all ;
While darkness deepens over Africa.
He turns to dearer themes—tells how he yearns
For home and his belovèd ; but would fain
Finish his work, since all the means are here.
" Nor will my labour now detain me long ! "
They pore upon their notes, and charts ; arrange

The future, lying on a fur-strewn floor,
By oil-light, burning in a shard for lamp;
Sipping black coffee, breathing fragrant fume . . .
With other heart and other hopes to-night
Livingstone hearkens to the solemn sound
Of Tanganika's melancholy wave;
And his friend hearkens; for he may not sleep,
Whose heart is buoyant with a wondering joy.

CANTO VII.

" UILD me a hut to die in!—nevermore
May I behold my land, or my be-
loved."
So spake the Master; for the end
was near;
Whom his dark silent followers obey.
For Livingstone, resuming his life-load   .
With a light heart, for all his years, and frame
Outworn with mighty labour and long pain,

Help'd even more the Mistress of his soul,
His dark and awful Mistress, Africa.
But that inveterate foe, the dire disease,[22]
Watching lynx-eyed for opportunity,
Found it, alas ! when, with a dwindling life,
The old, but still young-hearted traveller
Would flounder, as in manhood's vigorous prime,
Through foul morasses, many hours a day.
The foe sprang on him ; and he felt full well
Its gripe this time was mortal : then the flesh
Quail'd and rebell'd—let him but struggle home !
Homeward they hasten—life ebbing apace.
And first he rides ; but soon they carry him.
So when they have arrived at Muilala,
He bows the head—"A hut where I may die !"

Now all the mists of death pass over him :
Terrible pain, ill dreams ; with longings vain
For one glimpse of a loving face afar.
It is the hour of mortal agony.
Watchman ! will the terrible night soon pass ?
Then through the darkness mounts a bitter cry ;

As through more darkness upon Calvary
Rose a more bitter crying from the Lord.
   Gloomy the night and sullen; whose faint breath
Moans among grasses of a lonely hut;
While Bemba mourns with dying wave afar . .
. . . Behold! a dim procession slowly moves
Athwart the gloom! phantasmal Hero-forms,
Scarr'd as with thunder; marr'd, yet glorious;
Their pale brows aureoled with martyr-flame;
Lovers of men, sublime in suffering;
Patriots of all races and all time;
Christian confessors whom the world admires;
And some, whom none regarded, saving Heaven.
They are come to claim their brother; and the
      First
Seems like unto the lowly Son of God.

   "Strew grass upon the hut; for I am cold!"
And those dark silent followers obey.
But Majuahra kneels beside the bed;
Dark Majuahra, a young slave set free,
Kneels by a rude bed in a bough-built hut;

And while his tears fall on the wasted hand,
That never did a fellow-creature wrong,
But only wrought deliverance for all ;
After the fourth day of his coming there,
At solemn midnight, noble Livingstone,
Saying, in a low voice, " I am going home ! "
Quietly sleeping, enters into rest.
A lamp faint glimmers on the little slave,
As on those grand wan features of the dead . .
. . Daylight has dawn'd—the Conqueror is
     crown'd !

Then all consult what it were best to do.
And his true followers, whom he has loved,
And taught, and saved from bondage worse than
     death,
Who have shared his perils and long wanderings ;
Chumah, Hamoyda, Susi, and the rest ;
Resolve to bear away the dear remains,
Even to the coast—a thousand miles away !
That so the English may receive their Chief,
And bring him home—where he desired to be.

But fearing lest the village interpose,
They hide the truth of their commander's death;
And, building a high fence around a booth,
Bury the body's inner parts beneath
A shadowy tree, with solemn funeral rites;
Carving thereover name and date of death.
All that remains they reverently prepare
During twelve mournful days beneath the sun,
Embalming it with salt that purifies.
Last in rude bark of a great tree they bear him
Toward the isle of clove and cinnamon,[23]
Bulbul and orange, and pomegranate flower;
Carrying their dead Leader to the sea,
Who in glad triumph should have brought them
          there!

THE CARAVAN.

A solemn, strange, a holy Caravan!
When was the like thereof beheld by man?
Slow journeying from unconjectured lands,
Behold! they bear him in their gentle hands;
His dark youths bear him in the rude grey bark,

I

As though their burden were a holiest ark.
Embalm'd they bear him from the lands of Nile,
As men bore Israel, Abraham, erewhile.
Weary and weak, and faint and fallen ill,
Through desert, jungle, forest wild and still,
By lake, and dismal swamp, and rolling river,
Slowly their dark procession winds forever.
How would the Chief exult at every sight!
Alas! those eagle eyes are seal'd in night.
Behold them winding over hill and plain,
In storm, in sunshine, calm and hurricane!
And if they may not hide what thing they bear,
Men banish them with horror and wild fear,
Far from all human dwelling; nor will feed;
Nor furnish aught to fill their bitter need;
Assailing them with hindering word and deed.
But though their burden may not wake to cheer,
The Hero-Spirit hovers very near:
Upon them rests the holy Master's power:
His soul before them moves, a mighty tower!
They, and the body, rest beneath the stars,
Or moonèd ghostly-rainbow'd cloudy bars;

Until at length they hear the sounding sea,
In all the grandeur of Eternity !
A solemn, strange, a holy Caravan !
When was the like thereof beheld by man ?

Now waft him homeward in the gallant ship,
Expanding her white wings for a long flight !
It is not far from when we look'd for him.
In Maytime we had hoped to greet the sail,
Wafting our stainless conqueror to rest
In his own land, irradiate with love,
Wearing our well-earn'd honour on his brow.
Then bells would have peal'd over him, and flowers
Strewn his triumphant path, and shouts of joy
Have rent the summer air to welcome him.
So we have welcomed our victorious
Warriors yesterday from Africa—
And so alas ! have mourn'd the noble band,
Who, call'd by honour, gloriously died.

A sail is sighted—he is coming home.

But all fair colours of the many nations
In harbour, flying low from many a mast,
And minute guns, and muffled voice of bells,
With reverent silence of assembling throngs,
And mourning emblems in the public ways,
Mournfully tell of how the hero comes!

Now yet a little further carry him.
Westminster opens wide her ancient doors
For more illustrious dust to enter in.
Honour the noble Scottish weaver-boy,
The lowly-born illustrious Livingstone!
With solemn music we will leave him here,
Among the ashes of our mighty fallen.
Behold! world-honour'd Shades that haunt the
        fane,
Statesman, or monarch, poet, soldier, sage—
The while he moves along their awful line
To his own hallow'd English sepulchre;
From yon far forest of lone Muilala
Moves to more glorious glooms of Westminster—
Bend in a grand reverent humility

Before our stainless warrior of the cross ;
Uncursed of any humblest human soul ;
Blest and for ever to be blest by man ;
Foremost of all explorers ; Liberator
Of the dark continent, and all her sons !

Africa, and America, appear
His mighty mourners ; for a staunchest friend,
Stanley is here ; and here the slave set free,[24]
Who brought his noble master to the coast;
The Negro youth, who breathed our English words
Of faithful hope, words we are breathing now,
Over that heart entomb'd in Africa.
For though she hath restored some dust to us,
In life, in death, She claims to hold his heart !
. . . Hath he not died in her own awful arms ?
His sons and daughters in deep sable robed
Bear large white wreaths of blossom for his grave :
Yea, dark Death lies all buried and conceal'd
Under sweet emblems of immortal life !
Alas ! if he had come to us alive,
He might have gather'd violets to-day ;

Listening to our earliest nightingale
Under the woodland sprays of soft young green ;
But we have strewn spring flowers upon the bier
And we have wrought in white azaleas
A cross thereover ; while our kindly Queen
Has twined her delicate wreath for him ; and some
Lay fadeless amaranth, with roses rare,
And his own cherish'd palms of Africa,
Palms of the conqueror, upon his breast.
Now while those ashes slowly sink to rest,
All Europe, and his Country bending over ;
While solemn music soars with seraph plume ;
Pearly soft sun-rays, like sweet wings of doves,
Enter yon high clerestories, and abide
Athwart grey marrying fans of the dim ceiling :
So all we mourners, piers, and monuments,
Glow with a rainbow glory, as from Heaven.

Is it not better as the Lord hath will'd ?
On his own chosen battle-field he falls,
Still pressing forward, face toward the foe !
A martyr's death and tomb illume with light

His plain severe sublimity of life.
Could he have borne, who drank the liberal wind
Of deserts, like a lion or a pard,
Our stifling air of dull proprieties,
And pale decorum's mild monotony?
Who, with clear eyes on the Celestial Pole,
Loved, like an Arab, wandering wild and free!

While some surmise the dubious dim realm,[25]
Where he surrender'd to a sacred cause
His very life-breath in a life-long war,
Holds verily the furthest founts of Nile!

His death-cold hand unveils a Mystery,
Which all the unyielding ages from of old
Have shrouded in impenetrable gloom;
A darkness formidable from tongues confused
Of hydra-headed Error, breathing fear.
Champion of knowledge, and celestial love!
Conqueror of unconquerable Nile!
Mortal too bold! who dared to penetrate
That awful phantom-guarded Presence-chamber,

Where never mortal came !—there blinded fell,
All unaware of his own victory !

For here, between these very parallels,
Ancient Purânas of the Indian
Place Soma Giri ; whence a vast long lake
Amâra flows, Amâra " of the Gods,"
And from Amâra, Nile.

     Alas ! he died
Unknowing all the hopeful fruit that Frere[26]
Ripened from those indignant words of truth,
A lone old man, among Hell's legionaries,
Unquailing hurl'd against the slave-trader.
He learn'd stern Baker's wonderful campaign :
Now, peradventure, he hath learn'd the whole !

But if Columbus, voyaging forlorn,
Wandering ever in wan ways unknown
Of shoreless ocean toward the dying day,
Daring, presumptuous mortal ! to assail
Barriers Heaven piles against mankind :

If that Columbus, fronting desperate crews
Of mutinous men, with tranquil eyes unmoved
From all their high and visionary aim ;
Landing at last upon another world,
Conquer'd from chaos in the power of faith,
A blooming world, that seem'd the Paradise
Of our first parents in their innocence,
And proudly named Columbia to-day—
If he, the Navigator, lives for ever
In all men's green, and grateful memory ;
With Raleigh, Gama, Bruce, and Magelhaens—
Then surely shall our English Livingstone,
Honouring this our own tumultuous time ;
Heroic with immortal heroism,
That burns for ever in humanity ;
Rouse all the race unto a loftier life !

THE END.

NOTES.

NOTE 1.

T may be said by somebody that I have taken a liberty with the Mountains of the Moon. Let him that is without sin cast the first stone. Burton maintains that Ptolemy knew perfectly well what he was about in making a great range of mountains run east and west across Central Africa. It is even probable (from what Du Chaillu and others have seen) that snowy Kilimandjaro (Meru) and Kenia form its eastern limit, while Burton's Cameroons Mountain, with the mountains Du Chaillu saw, form its western. But, at any rate, the most recent discoveries seem to indicate that the Karagwé highlands also send out branches southward. These flank Tanganyika, and run down to the west of

Lake Bangweolo or Bemba, afterwards trending off
again south of the same lake to enclose lakes Nyassa
and Shirwa (see Keith Johnstone's Map of Livingstone's
discoveries). The high plateau of Lobisa, where the
river Chambezi probably takes its rise, may on this
view be considered as belonging to the same system.
But there are north and south coast ranges inosculating
with these latitudinal mountains—while possibly neither
Abyssinian highlands on the one hand, nor heights
enclosing Albert Nyanza on the other, ought to be
regarded as cut off from them. Where Livingstone's
" four fountains of Herodotus " (which he was so keen
to find) are, seems indeed to be still a moot point—like
most matters connected with Central African geography.

2. Livingstone's discoveries remarkably confirmed
Sir R. Murchison's theories as to the geological con-
dition of South Africa—for he found no evidences of
marine formations, which would be found if the land
had been submerged, as other continents have been, since
the oldest secondary era of geologists. In his books
may be read his statements of fact, and his inferences
on these matters. The great lakes that, at the time of
the deposition of the oldest secondary strata, were
much larger than at present, have been let out, he

believes, by fissures suddenly opened in the flanking ranges, as at the Falls of Mosi-oa-tunya. See Murchison on the Physical Geography of Inner Africa.—Journal R. Geog. Society, 1864.

3. In Manyuema, west of Tanganyika, where Livingstone has been, the huts are built almost entirely of ivory; while in Ashantee gold is profusely employed.

4. Du Chaillu ; and Schweinfurth, the record of whose very remarkable and daring explorations have been recently published. I am of course aware that Livingstone did not really know of the latter. It is indeed sad to think how near the two travellers were to one another when both were turned back.

5. I do not deem this inconsistent with Livingstone's large, though reverent and evangelical, utterance respecting the death of Sebituane. (See "Missionary Travels.")

6. A bird of Ashantee with brilliant red plumage. This vision is suggested by descriptions given of African races that practise human sacrifice—*e. g.* those of Ashantee and Dahomey.

7. The negroes can hardly conceive of death, in the case of young persons, without supposing it brought about by some malignant enchantment. They believe themselves surrounded by all kinds of spiritual

agencies, good and bad—and, though their ideas about spiritual matters are vague and variable enough, they are often found to hold a somewhat crude form of the doctrine of transmigration.

8. The medicine-man or magician is relied on to point out who have bewitched the dead—which affords him ample scope for malignity. He makes each victim drink the ordeal poison (various plants are used—the *Muave*, the *Mboundou*, &c.) ; then if the poison takes effect, the popular voice decides that the person is truly guilty, and the tribe despatch him or her with knives. It is said that the old rascal has some secret, by the knowledge of which he renders the poison innocuous to himself.

9. This anecdote is told in Livingstone's first great book of missionary travels—and it was by the imperfectly-healed fracture of the bone of his left arm that the remains brought over to England were identified on their arrival as those of Livingstone ; Sir W. Ferguson making the examination in the presence of the Rev. Dr. Moffat, Dr. Kirk, Mr. Webb of Newstead, and Mr. Waller, who had formerly seen Livingstone's injured arm.

10. This dog the traveller seems to have procured on his last voyage. Mr. Young, in his " Search for

Livingstone," says that he heard of this dog at a village where he arrived; and where he gained such information as assured him of the falsehood of the traitor Musa's fabricated report respecting Livingstone's murder by the Ma-Zitu—said to have taken place in 1866. Sir R. Murchison, doubting the report, as President of the Royal Geographical Society, together with the Council, sent out Mr. E. Young to ascertain the truth. He proved a most competent leader. The native woman who spoke of this dog said, laughing, "it seemed to have two tails"—and the Rev. Mr. Waller afterwards suggested an explanation of this to Mr. Young; relating how Livingstone (ever fond of a joke) had disputed the fact alleged by learned men, that every dog under domestication still retains the tendency of a wild dog's tail to curl to the left, and complained that he was always obliged now, whenever he heard a dog bark, to march out of his way in order to examine his tail! Mr. Waller further suggested that Livingstone had picked up a dog, whose tail curled to the *right;* and that this controversy being explained to the natives, they made a hash of it, saying the dog Chitani seemed to have two tails.

11. At St. Paul de Loanda, the Portuguese settlement on the West Coast.

12. Mrs. Livingstone died at Shupanga, whither

she had come from England to join her husband for the second time—having before gone with him, after their marriage, from Kuruman (Moffat's station) to Kolobeng; and after residing with him there as a missionary's wife, having travelled with him and some of their children to Lake Ngami, across the Kalahari desert, when the children greatly suffered. In the lyric that follows I have to acknowledge some obligation to a pretty poem in a small life of the traveller, published by Messrs. Hodder and Stoughton. Bishop Mackenzie and Rev. Mr. Burrup are alluded to.

13. The Makololo chief, Sekeletu, and his people, furnished Livingstone with the means necessary to enable him to go from Linyanti to the west coast, and afterwards to the east. Without these "niggers," *who urged him and helped him to explore*—to open a highway for commerce and Christianity—he could have done nothing.

14. This was the little ship Livingstone built with the £6000 derived from the sale of his first book; for the steamer sent by Government did not answer his purpose of exploring the Zambesi and Shirè. This sum, as Stanley tells us, in his latest edition of "How I Found Livingstone," the traveller lost. Having crossed to Bombay in his little craft—a marvellous feat—he

sold her for £2000; but lost this afterwards through the bankruptcy of the banker with whom it was deposited.

15. See Irving's " Life of Columbus."

16. A kind of cuckoo, so called by the natives.

17. This was before Stanley explored the north of Tanganyika with Livingstone, and found the Rusizi river to be an influent.   If there should be an effluent in the direction of the Kabogo mountains, to the west, this might join the Lualaba ; and so possibly (according to Livingstone's theory), the Nile.   Perhaps Lieutenant Cameron, now at Ujiji, will discover this.   But Schweinfurth's discoveries seem to prove that this could only be by way of the Albert Nyanza ; not by way of Petherick's branch, the Bahr el Ghazal.

18. Named by Livingstone "Victoria Falls."   The native name signifies "sounding smoke."   Mr. Oswell, who was with Livingstone when he first discovered the cataract, and had seen Niagara, gave the palm to Mosi-oa-tunya.   The *Mowana* is the gigantic *Baobab* tree of Africa.   The *Mohonono* tree is said to be like a cedar, and the *Motsouri* like a cypress.   For a full account of the falls, see Livingstone's two books of travel.   The water (of the river Zambesi, or Leeambayee) clears a moment as it falls, becomes a sheet of foam, or rather a sheet of *comets* of foam, separate from one another, with

nucleus and tail. This phenomenon is apparently very remarkable; though I think I remember to have observed something like it in the falls of the Rhine. The "Evergreen Grove" is on a ledge of rock opposite the fall. But "Garden Island," where the travellers made a garden, is on the same side.

19. Ntanda, a native name for the planet Venus, meaning *firstborn.*

20. The Bakwain chief, with whom Livingstone resided at Kolobeng. For an account of Africaner, see the Rev. Dr. Moffat's "Missionary Travels."

21. Mr. Young, of Kelly, a true friend to Livingstone, without whose private generosity he could not have carried forward his great labours.

22. Dysentery was the disease to which he was subject, and of which he died (1873). The precise locality where he died seems almost strangely vague.

23. Zanzibar.

24. Jacob Wainwright, a negro slave, educated at Nassick College, near Bombay, came over in the "Malwa" with his master's remains, and attended the funeral in Westminster Abbey. He read some of the English service over those parts of the body that were buried under the tree at Muilala, or Ilala. He was sent up to the Doctor from Zanzibar by Mr. Stanley, with other

K

valuable men, as soon as the latter reached the coast—
Livingstone having resolved to wait for them and other
necessary supplies at Unyanyembe.

25. If in Lobisa the Chambezi rises—which is the
same river that flows out of Lake Bangweolo or Bemba as
the Luapula; which again, on issuing from Lake Moero,
becomes Lualaba—and if the Lualaba send one branch
to the Congo, and another to the Nile—then this claim
may be made for the presumed whereabouts of Livingstone's death.   On the other hand, Mr. Findlay still
maintains (unless I mistake) with Sir S. Baker and
Captain Burton, that Tanganyika is virtually the same
as Albert Nyanza; or has an effluent north, which joins
the latter.   But as Livingstone died somewhere near the
southern feeders of Lake Liemba, which is the same
lake as Tanganyika, even on this view, the same claim
can be made.

26. It is to be hoped that the provisions of Sir
Bartle Frere's treaty, concluded with the Sultan of
Zanzibar, which we owe to Livingstone's fearless re-
presentations by letter of the slave-trading horrors he
witnessed on his last journey, will be faithfully carried
out, and that England will see that they are.

CHISWICK PRESS:—PRINTED BY WHITTINGHAM AND WILKINS,
TOOKS COURT, CHANCERY LANE.

THE RED FLAG.

AND OTHER POEMS,

BY THE HON. RODEN NOEL.

AUTHOR OF "BEATRICE AND OTHER POEMS."

Small 8vo, 6s.

" There are poetry and power of a high order in the volume before us The 'Red Flag' is a terrible and thunderous poem. There are fine sympathies with the sorrows of London life and wonderful knowledge of them. Perhaps one of the most solemn, awful poems of the present century is ' The Vision of the Desert.' . . . Let his imagination and metaphysical faculty be well yoked and guided by his own cultivated taste, and we must all admit the advent of a great poet."—*British Quarterly Review.*

" Mr. Noel's new volume marks a decided advance both in clearness of form and in melody of expression upon his earlier collection. He has succeeded in working out more unity of style, in harmonizing his thought and feeling, and in producing more sustained effects of music in verse without sacrificing individuality. . . . It is probably upon the compositions of the third and fourth sections that the reputation of Mr. Noel as a poet of marked originality will ultimately rest. The situation of ' The Red Flag' is finely conceived and powerfully presented. The sincerity of the poet, his intense feeling for the terrible, the realism with which he has wrought every detail of his picture, and his passionate sympathy with the oppressed, make the general effect of this poem very impressive. In ' Palingenesis' and 'Richmond Hill' and the ' Sea Symphony' Mr. Noel exhibits a rarer quality of artistic production. These poems are steeped in thought and feeling : Nature is represented with the most minute and patient accuracy, yet each description is pervaded with a sense of the divine mysterious life that throbs within the world. We need to travel back to the Bhagavadgita or to take Walt Whitman from the shelf if we seek to match the pantheistic enthusiasm of the climax to ' Palingenesis.' The promise of Mr. Noel's earlier poem in this style, ' Pan,' is here fulfilled." —*Academy.*

" There is much unpalatable truth in this satire, sometimes very cleverly put. . . . . We do not think any lover of poetry can read ' The Water-Nymph and the Boy,' ' Allerheiligen,' or ' Palingenesis,' without enjoying and admiring the exquisitely coloured word-pictures they contain."—*Scotsman.*

" A volume of very remarkable poems. There are a richness of thought, a power of language, a wild, rushing, cataract-like movement of melody, and an originality of purpose almost unique among the rising poets of the age, in this volume. It will be Mr. Noel's own fault if he does not take the very highest rank among his contemporary poets."—*Dundee Advertiser.*

" A singular book, in which there is much real poetic force and feeling."— *Graphic.*

" Our skeleton sketch gives little notion of the earnest power of this noble poem. . . . The volume will reach and please a wider circle than the last, and we believe that future volumes will soon make the writer's name familiar to all appreciative readers of good English poetry."—*Weekly Review.*

" The lines we have italicised seem to us to be worthy of the very foremost of our living poets."—*Freeman.*

" The writer has more than that love of nature which spends itself on the beauty of form and colour ; he is alive to that more spiritual emotion which connects the aspects of outward nature with the aspirations of the human soul. . . . In spite of these faults, he is capable on occasions of writing noble passages."—*Spectator.*

" In striking contrast to the tone and manner and rhythm of the opening poem is the succeeding one, entitled ' April Gleams.' It is dainty as gossamer, fanciful, dreamy, suggestive of summer melodies and woodland brooks."— *Morning Post.*

MEMOIR OF DR. LIVINGSTONE.

BY H. M. STANLEY.

See

HOW I FOUND LIVINGSTONE.

This Edition contains all the Small and some of the Large
Illustrations, and a long Introductory Chapter on the Death
of Livingstone, with a brief Memoir, and Extracts from
Dr. Livingstone's last Correspondence with Mr. Stanley, now
first published.

7s. 6d., crown 8vo., cloth extra, uniform with the Cheap
Edition of Major Butler's " The Great Lone Land." &c.

This Edition has been revised most carefully from beginning to
end, and all matter of a personal or irrelevant character omitted.

N.B.—Copies of the Original Edition, cloth extra, gilt edges,
may be had, 10s. 6d.

A few Extracts from Press Notices:—

" The freshness with which Mr. Stanley writes, his real powers of
narrative and description, his quick observation and very industrious
collection of materials, all going hand in hand as they do with the reader's
keen interest in the subject, with admiration of the courage, energy, self-
reliance, and ready resource of the traveller, and with the strange, semi-
chivalrous, semi-commercial nature of his mission, render the work he has
so soon published excellent reading."—*The Times.*

" The book is admirably illustrated, and the whole story of adventure
and discovery is so well told that we go along with the author in his explorations, realise his dangers, feel the very climate of Africa to be around
us, and are almost able to see Dr. Livingstone himself at work."—*Daily
News.*

" It would be impossible within the narrow limits of a first notice, to
attempt to convey an adequate idea of the thousand and one topics of
interest dealt with in this volume."—*Morning Post.*

" Mr. Stanley's book may be pronounced thoroughly interesting and
valuable. His feat was so successful in its results, and was besides so
admirably well managed in every detail, that it must stand out in all time
coming as exceptional in the records of African travel."—*Daily Telegraph.*

" It is needless to recommend a book like this, which is certain to be
eagerly devoured by every one who can get hold of it ; we will, therefore,
only say that Mr. Stanley's pen is as facile and flowing as his heart is
courageous, and that the story of his adventures, perils, and final triumph
in his search after Livingstone suffers no drawback from any tediousness
or clumsiness in the telling."—*Graphic.*

" We know of no book of African travel which has a better story to tell,
and few which, on the whole, tell their story more graphically .... his
book well deserves reading."—*Saturday Review.*

LONDON: SAMPSON LOW, MARSTON, LOW AND SEARLE,

CROWN BUILDINGS, 188, FLEET STREET, E.C.